FAKE FACTS

★ BY THE ★

BATHROOM READERS' INSTITUTE

BATHROOM READERS' PRESS

ASHLAND, OREGON

"Now, what I want is, Facts. Teach these boys and girls nothing but Facts. Facts alone are wanted in life. Plant nothing else, and root out everything else. You can only form the minds of reasoning animals upon Facts: nothing else will ever be of any service to them. This is the principle on which I bring up my own children, and this is the principle on which I bring up these children. Stick to Facts, sir!"

—Charles Dickens, *Hard Times* (1854)

"Half of everything I ever said was lies, the other half I totally made up."

—Abraham Lincoln, on his blog (2004)

UNCLE JOHN'S BATHROOM READER®
FAKE FACTS

For information, write:
The Bathroom Readers' Institute, P.O. Box 1117,
Ashland, OR 97520
www.bathroomreader.com

Cover and interior design by Andy Taray / Ohioboy.com

ISBN-13: 978-1-60710-559-6 / ISBN-10: 1-60710-559-6

Library of Congress Cataloging-in-Publication Data

Uncle John's bathroom reader fake facts.
p. cm.
ISBN 978-1-60710-559-6 (pbk.)
1. Curiosities and wonders – Humor. 2. American wit and humor. I.
Bathroom Readers' Institute (Ashland, Or.)
PN6165.U523 2012
818'.602–dc23
2012009289

Printed in United States of America
First Printing: September 2012
17 16 15 14 13 12 6 5 4 3 2 1

THANK YOU!

The Bathroom Readers' Institute sincerely thanks the people
whose advice and assistance made this book possible.

Gordon Javna

Brian Boone

Sharilyn Carroll

Jay Newman

Andy Taray

Christy Taray

Claudia Bauer

Brandon Hartley

Eleanor Pierce

Megan Todd

Michael Conover

Kim Griswell

Trina Janssen

David Hoye

Jennifer Frederick

Sydney Stanley

Lillian Nordland

Melinda Allman

JoAnn Padgett

True Sims

Andy Kaufman

Thomas "Fuller" Crapper

CONTENTS

LET'S FAKE MAGIC!

For more than 25 years here at the Bathroom Readers' Institute, we've scoured the library, poured over newspapers, and braved the Internet to find interesting stories and true facts to share with you, dear reader, in a fun, engaging way. It's actually really hard. So what do trivia writers do to cut loose? We invent *untrue* facts, just to make ourselves laugh ("Brunch was invented by John Brunchman!" "It's a felony to carry live flowers in Allentown, Pennsylvania!" "Tolstoy wrote a sequel to *War and Peace* set on Mars!"). It was so much fun that we decided to do a whole book of them in the hope that you'll find them funny, too.

You'll find in *Fake Facts* what you usually find in an Uncle John's book: origin stories, slang terms, historical moments, product failures, and more…the only difference is that absolutely *none of it is true*. (Well, not on purpose. If we stumbled onto something real, trust us—it's a complete accident.) Read all about:

• Why pirates kept parrots. (They thought they carried pirate souls)

• *When Harry Met Sally,* and other forgotten video games

• How to make an artificial kidney

This book really gave us a chance to play up the sarcasm and wit that are present in every Bathroom Reader…but without having to use a fact-checker. We hope you have as good a time fun reading it as we did writing it. And that's the truth.

—Uncle John and the Bathroom Readers' Institute

21 ANIMAL GROUPING NAMES

A pretty of ponies

A foreboding of canaries

A scarlet of cardinals

A debbie of gibbons

A bucket of chicken

A deliciousness of cows

A jerk of goats

A proxy of ghosts

A magical of unicorns

A foul of foals

A sadness of narwhals

A blank of Tasmanian devils

A ripken of orioles

A traffic of deer

A wily of coyotes

A buffalo of buffalo

A waddle of penguins

A pancake of Gila monsters

A rodeo of bulls

A rack of yellow jackets

A bunch of dogs

VIDEO GAME FLOPS

Mario Book 64 (1998)

Nintendo produced this "educational" title featuring Mario reading books. Players turn the page with the controller, but never get to see the text as Mario reads it, although he occasionally shouts out "Mamma mia!" at "the good parts."

Websurferz (1995)

It stars Boardz, an anthropomorphic surfboard, as he "surfs" the Internet and learns about proper chat room safety and Web etiquette, or "Netiquette."

Sim-Deity (1992)

The player literally "plays God" as a deity which designs the universe. Video game fans praised the game's difficulty—it's entirely in ancient Hebrew and requires relentless, rapid decision-making.

Lion! (1997)

The player controls a lion. To properly study and incorporate lion behavior, designers lived among a pride in Kenya. Three team members were mauled on the first day of the study, at which point where designers were allowed only to watch lions in a zoo. Result: The game features a lot of lions sitting around, pacing, and waiting to be fed.

STRANGE MEDICAL CONDITIONS

Wrong Foot Disease

A neurological condition in which the "wires are crossed" to the feet—the brain tries to control the left foot, but the right foot ends up moving, and vice versa. Those with WFD can learn to walk and move after extensive physical therapy and practice.

Diner Urine Disease

Due to a buildup of a specific group of proteins in the bladder, people with DUD have urine that smells just like a diner, a distinct combination of bacon, cigarette smoke, coffee, and Lysol.

Double Liver

DL patients have a liver that is twice the size of a normal, adult-size liver. How is it treated? By strategically shrinking the extra tissue into oblivion—patients are ordered to drink upwards of 10 servings of alcohol per day.

Opposite Fluid Disbursement

Physiologically speaking, earwax and snot are not all that different, and both serve to protect—earwax protects the ears, and snot (or mucus) protects the nose from germs. Except if you have opposite fluid disbursement, in which mucus grows in the ears, and earwax forms in the nose.

FORGOTTEN FAD: MOON PARLORS

Atlanta businessman Aldous Johnson, who made his fortune as one of the original founders of the Burger Chef restaurant chain, was, like the rest of the United States in 1969, caught up in "moon fever." The Space Age was in full force, with *Apollo* astronauts landing on the moon in July 1969. In early 1970, Johnson opened up a chain of 29 Apollo Moon Parlors in major American cities. Quaint by today's standards, the moon parlors were housed in converted warehouses—high ceilings were fitted with sparkling lights to look like stars, a mural of the distant Earth was painted on a wall, green-costumed "moon men" wandered around, and kids got to bounce on a trampoline-like "antigravity moon surface," similar to today's bounce houses.

The parlors were a huge hit—they made Johnson $25 million between 1970 and 1972. But as moon missions became routine, moon fever died down, and attendance at Apollo Moon Parlors dropped. The chain closed by the end of 1972.

THE ORIGIN OF CANNED TUNA

A massive international scandal erupted in the late 1980s when news broke that thousands of dolphins a year were being accidentally caught and killed by giant nets trolling the oceans for tuna. It led to a revamp of how tuna were caught in order to protect the endangered dolphins, with a "dolphin-safe" logo created to let consumers know that canned tuna was friendly to the sea mammal. What most consumers don't know is that the tuna industry only began after commercial dolphin fishing was exhausted in the 1930s. Companies like Dolphincrest and Sea Cow sold more than a billion cans of dolphin each year between 1925 and 1937. But by 1940, they'd exhausted dolphins to near extinction. So fisheries decided to start going after the large, meaty fish that they'd been throwing out when they routinely got caught in dolphin-fishing nets: tuna.

CANADA FACTS

• Canada is larger than the United States, Brazil, and Russia put together.

• The idea of Canada being cold and snowy isn't true, at least for the major, southernmost cities. It snowed 25 days in Toronto in 2010. Vancouver hasn't had a snowfall since 2006.

• Most Americans know that Canadians enjoy government-paid health care. What else is "socialized" in Canada? The government pays for cable TV (but not premium channels like HBO), garbage service, and health care for pets. To cut down on paper consumption, in 2011 the government issued every Canadian adult a free book e-reader and a $50 gift card to fill them up.

• Canada is a lot like the U.S., but with a few major differences. For example, dogs are a popular pet there. Cats, however, never quite caught on. While in the U.S., the ratio of dog households to cat households hovers around 1:1, in Canada, the ratio of dog households to cat households is an astounding 15:1.

• Canadians prefer homegrown movies. Of the 100 top-grossing films of all time in Canada, only two were American-made: *Titanic* and *Dick Tracy*.

THE PRESIDENTIAL ORDER OF SUCCESSION, FARTHER DOWN THE LINE

In the event of a catastrophe that rendered the U.S. president and vice president unable to lead, there's a presidential order of succession. The list goes far deeper than the 18 positions (speaker of the House of Representatives, cabinet secretaries, etc.) commonly listed in trivia books.

#19 Prime minister of Canada

#20 American with the largest personal collection of guns

#21 Sitting host of *The Tonight Show*

#22 Oldest living American

#23 Tallest living American

#24 The King of Rock n' Roll (amended by Congress in 1978 to "The Boss"—Bruce Springsteen)

#25 President of the Future Farmers of America

#26 MVP of the most recent Super Bowl

#27 Recipient of the most recent Academy Award for Best Director

#28 Winner of the most recent "Why I Would Make a Good President" national junior-high essay contest

#29 Living American with the most friends on Facebook

#30 Winner of the most recent Powerball jackpot

#31 Ryan Seacrest

ORIGINAL TV PILOT PREMISES

Charlie's Angels

The popular '70s series followed three female secret agents—a new concept in TV portrayals of gender. The pilot episode was one of the most convoluted projects in TV history—nine separate teams of three "angels" worked on a single case, for a total of 27 actresses. It was even more confusing because two sets of twins and one set of triplets were in the cast (but none were on the same team as their siblings), while an additional four characters were all named Samantha.

Mork and Mindy

It began as *Mark and Mindy*, a generic sitcom about a young couple that slowly falls in love. Then producers cast comedian Robin Williams as Mark. He showed them a routine from his stage act in which he portrayed a wacky alien. "Mark" quickly became "Mork," a wacky alien, and the show became *Mork and Mindy*.

7th Heaven

This light drama ran for 10 seasons with the simple premise: A minister tends to his flock, and raises his family of seven children. In the pilot screened for WB Network executives, the show took its title literally: it took place in Heaven. The series would have been about the family adjusting to life in the afterlife.

Hill Street Blues

Steven Bochco pitched the idea to NBC as a gritty police drama…intercut with fully-animated, Disney-style production numbers. NBC made him take out the songs and cartoon bits.

MacGyver

ABC bought the idea of a secret agent who never resorts to violence, relying instead on his ability to solve cases using ingenious gadgets made out of common materials. The marketing department of Amway conceived the show, and it ran for seven years with the concept mostly intact, losing only the element of *MacGyver* making lifesaving inventions exclusively out of Amway products.

Star Trek

The thoughtful, allegorical plots and intricate science-fiction framework were part of the pilot episode, but creator Gene Roddenberry's initial concept was for an entirely female cast, all dressed in miniskirts and go-go boots. NBC thought the outfits were too scandalous and hated Roddenberry's working title: *Go-Go Groovy Space Chicks!*

Mister Ed

It was always about a talking horse, but in the original script, only Wilbur could hear Ed talk, and even then only in his mind. Problem: The audience couldn't hear the horse talking either.

FOLK MEDICINE FROM AROUND THE WORLD

• Before the advent of vaccinations (and even after), parents in the Basque region in Europe protected their children against illnesses with a week spent in a hammock made from the wool of their village's oldest sheep.

• An old Mongolian practice for curing vision problems called for collecting the dirt from where "three dogs marked the same spot," then brewing it piping hot.

• Freckles are common on redheaded, fair-skinned Irish people, who long ago had an old folk remedy for removing them: Apply the flame of a moss fire directly to—and only to—the freckles.

• After Gutenberg perfected the printing press in Germany in the 15th century, it was heralded as a miracle. So much so that Germans believed that taking a printed pamphlet into the bathroom with them would alleviate constipation.

• Fishing villages in feudal Japan believed that wearing a necklace made of fish bones would ease arthritis pain.

• Ancient Egyptians fed arthritic cats a diet of banana peels and apple juice.

• A home remedy from the American South: Simmer a pot of apple cider vinegar for an hour, then soak your fingers in the vinegar. Result: No more hangnails.

• Knights in medieval England ate a concoction of mustard, relish, and sand before every jousting competition, as it was thought to bring "good luck and great vigor," as noted in Chaucer's *The Canterbury Tales*.

• To many people in India, cows are sacred…but left-handedness is an abomination. The cure: If a cow steps on an acai berry, the left-handed individual must eat the berry in order to cure the affliction.

• A bracelet made of silk, human hair, and gold thread was said to protect ancient Arabian travelers from bandits.

• To ease growing pains in the joints of adolescents, people in early Scandinavia would tightly bind the entire body for one full cycle of the moon.

• From colonial New England: To cure a stammer, chew eight raw coffee beans until they are liquefied, then spit them out to the north.

• Medieval French doctors believed that inhaling the smoke from burning unicorn hair prevented demonic possession.

SECRET MESSAGES IN FAMOUS SONGS

Frank Sinatra, "I Get a Kick Out of You" (1954)

Sinatra is responsible for what's widely believed to be the first "backmasked" (reverse-recorded) message in a widely released LP. At the 1:31 mark of "I Get a Kick Out of You," the song rolls into a brassy interlude. If you play this portion of the track in reverse and listen closely, you'll hear Sinatra read his favorite recipe for hot chocolate: "You've gotta use two small marshmallows, doll. Three's too many, one's too few."

The Beatles, "While My Guitar Gently Weeps" (1968)

John Lennon's hidden "turn me on, dead man" blurb in "Revolution # 9" attracted plenty of attention in the late '60s and fueled rumors of Paul McCartney's death. But another concealed message on *The White Album* is all but forgotten and may have even added to the tensions surrounding the band's breakup. During the piano riff that opens George Harrison's pop masterpiece, the "Quiet Beatle" included the following broken limerick: "There once was a bloke from Liverpool, who played in a band of irritable fools, he was often overlooked, and they were overcooked, so he'll quit if you fans don't tell him not to." This odd plea for encouragement was ignored; the Beatles were history two years later.

Led Zeppelin, "Stairway to Heaven" (1971)

Parent groups spent a good chunk of their time in the early

'80s decrying the alleged inclusion of evil backward messages in rock songs, particularly the supposed chant of "here's to my sweet Satan" in the guitar solo of Led Zeppelin's most famous song. The ears of Zeppelin's critics were playing tricks on them. The actual message hidden in "Stairway to Heaven" can be heard at the 0:29 mark of the song. Played backward, the listener hears John Paul Jones speak the praises of a high fiber diet. He repeats the words "stay regular" twice.

Prince, "Computer Blue" (1984)

During the synthesizer diminuendo at the 2:16 mark of this *Purple Rain* cut, there's a quick series of barely audible beeps. If this sequence is reversed and filtered through spectrographic software, an image of a camel appears in the visualized sound waves. Why it was included remains a mystery. Over a decade later, Aphex Twin included a similarly hidden image—of a monkey—inside the song "Windowlicker."

The London Symphony Orchestra, "The Meadow" (from the *Twilight: New Moon* soundtrack, 2009)

Film composer Alexandre Desplat included a raunchy recording in the middle of the orchestral "The Meadow," from the soundtrack to the second *Twilight* movie. If you turn your stereo up loud, you'll hear the sounds of passionate lovemaking as the violins fade at the end of the track. In a 2010 interview with *Diapason*, a French classical music magazine, Desplat confessed that he and "a lusty trombonist" made the recording late one night in the orchestra's studio.

FAILED AMUSEMENT PARKS

Kenny World

During a career slump in the mid-1980s, country singer Kenny Rogers asked Dolly Parton, his frequent duet partner, for investment advice. Parton's recommendation: Do what she did, and open an amusement park. Using Dollywood as a model, Rogers opened up Kenny World in Sugar Land, Texas, a suburb of his hometown of Houston. There were rides and attractions based on several of Rogers's songs and movies, including The Coward of the County Junior Roller Coaster, The Gambler's Old Timey Saloon (which featured an animatronic cowboy fight), and the Islands in the Stream Log Flume Extravaganza. Rogers performed at the park one night a month, and all food services were handled by Kenny Rogers Roasters, the chicken franchise Rogers owned. The park brought in more than 500,000 visitors a year from its opening in 1987 until 1992. It closed in 1993 due to safety violations and lawsuits resulting from patrons injured on the Drop In to See What Condition Your Condition Is In ride, a tower-drop style ride which included a 300-foot, 60 mph free fall…and subpar harnesses. Occupying the site today is a golf course owned by country star Charlie Daniels.

Euro Knott's Berry Farm

When Disney announced in 1991 that it was going to build an amusement park in a planned community near Paris, the eventual success of "Euro Disney" was considered a lock. It wasn't nearly as successful as Disneyland or Disney World, much to the chagrin of Knott's Berry Farm, which sought to latch on to what it thought would be a huge cash windfall by building another branch of its theme park franchise next door to Euro Disney. (The original Knott's Berry Farm is just down the road from Disneyland in California.) Euro Knott's Berry Farm was a huge flop—the French had no connection to the rural American farm atmosphere of KBF, nor did they have any knowledge of the Peanuts characters used as the park's mascots. A switch to the 1950s French comic strip character Lil Charlemagne didn't help—the park went out of business in 1994.

Six Flags Over Alaska/Six Flags Over Russia

In 1992 the Cold War was over, and for the first time in decades, there was peace, even friendship, between the United States and the former Soviet Union. The Six Flags theme park chain wanted to build on that goodwill and literally link the two nations with a pair of amusement parks: one located on Little Diomede, a remote Alaskan island that is just two miles from the easternmost Russian island of Big Diomede…which is where the second park would go. Visitors would travel freely from park to park (provided they had passports and could handle a 45-minute barge ride). The parks were only partially built when planners realized that snow and ice covered both islands for 10 months out of the year, and that it would take more than 10 hours to fly in tourists from the closest major mainland airport in Seattle.

COCKTAIL ORIGINS

Screwdriver

Created in eastern Europe in the 1940s, the drink gets its name because vodka at the time, in that part of the world, came shipped in aluminum cans, not bottles. The only way to get one open was to puncture the top with a screwdriver.

White Russian

Cocaine was legal to buy, use, and sell in the United States until 1938. It was particularly popular in Boston, where Russian grocers and pharmacists kept the drug in stock. Because of that, and the fact that it's a white powder, cocaine was known in the Boston area as "white Russian." When cocaine was banned, a local bartender whipped up a concoction of cream, coffee liqueur, and vodka. Because it both intoxicated and rejuvenated, he said the drink was just as good as "white Russian." The name stuck.

Shirley Temple

The parents and agent of 1930s child actress Francesca L. Krzyzewski thought the young girl would never get any roles with such a long, difficult-to-pronounce name. While talking about the problem at dinner one night, the five-year-old actress ordered a popular non-alcoholic drink consisting of ginger ale, grenadine, and orange juice, called a Temple Cocktail after the Los Angeles haunt the Temple Bar and Grill. The waitress asked the child's parents if that was okay, and her father responded, "Well, surely." The agent immediately got an idea, changed the spelling around, and soon "Shirley Temple" was on her way to success.

Cape Cod

It was originally called a Cape Codder. Made up of vodka and cranberry juice, the drink was invented by coastal Massachusetts bartender Thomas Cape, and it initially included the area's biggest export: cod (salted cod, specifically). So many customers ordered the drink without the cod that Cape eventually stopped stocking the fish, serving the drink with just the other two ingredients.

CITY NICKNAME ORIGINS

Chicago, "The Windy City"

It's a much newer nickname than you'd think. In 1967 the band The Association had a #1 hit with "Windy," but it was dispro-portionately, hugely popular in the Chicago area, selling three million copies to a population of just over four million people. Warner Bros. Records thanked Chicago for its support (al-though evidence suggests WBR was given kickbacks by the mob-run Chicago record store racket) with full-page magazine ads labeling Chicago "The 'Windy' City."

New York City, "The Big Apple"

In 1927 *New York Telegraph* columnist John F. Fitzgerald wrote an article about how the city was "a festering stinkhole of crime and garbage, diseased beyond hope" due to political corruption. "While things taste sweet from the halls of Wall Street or the bright lights of Broadway, at the center of this city, is a fierce, impenetrable, and impossible to digest core, rotting this big apple from the inside out."

Seattle, "The Emerald City"

The first structures in the city were elaborate towers carved out of the naturally occurring emerald cliffs that once over-looked Puget Sound. By 1910 all the emeralds—including the ones making up the Emerald Towers—had been mined and shipped to Asia.

Boston, "Beantown"

In the early 17th century, Boston was first settled by a sect of pilgrims who, for religious reasons, didn't eat meat. As vegetarians often do today, the pilgrims relied on large volumes of beans as a protein source.

Paris, "The City of Light"

Until 1915 the city was an optical illusion created by prisms, mirrors, and powerful light beams emanating from the home of famous magician Francois "Le Magnifique" Duchamp. To this day, it's not known exactly how he made an entire, gigantic, major world city and its residents appear real.

Portland, "Bridgetown"

Seattle and San Francisco were big trading ports in the early 20th century. To connect them, developers installed an elevated canal between the two cities, with a way station in the middle. That way station, "Bridgetown," eventually developed into Portland.

Philadelphia, "The City of Brotherly Love"

The city was the birthplace of the Lawrence brothers—Joey, Matthew, and Andrew Lawrence, who have appeared on sitcoms such as *Boy Meets World* and *Blossom*. The three starred together on *Brotherly Love* (1995–97), which was filmed in Philadelphia, prompting then-mayor Ed Rendell to proclaim Philadelphia "the city of *Brotherly Love.*"

THE LOST WORKS OF WILLIAM SHAKESPEARE

In 1979 a weathered leather dossier was discovered in a private library in Sydney, Australia. The initials "W.S." were embossed upon it, and it was filled with half-finished plays, notes, and sonnets, suggesting that the file contained previously unknown works of William Shakespeare.

Arthur of Britannia. The legends surrounding King Arthur and Camelot inspired the first project the playwright ever tackled, while he was still a teenager. This incomplete, 69-page script concludes suddenly with an 800-word soliloquy by Sir Lancelot, in which the knight verbosely and explicitly longs for Queen Guinevere's "radiant bosom." Merlin the Wizard is described as "quite flatulent with a mystical fart wand" and the rest of the script is mostly fight scenes, cheesy double-entendres, and "thy mother" jokes.

A Mid-autumn Night's Plague. Centered around the wedding of Duke Adonis of Athens and the mysterious Queen Yeoh, it takes place in the 14th century during the height of the Black Death that decimated Europe. Shakespeare blames the plague, which infects and kills most of the characters in the third act, on a plot orchestrated by a lovesick sprite. Perhaps reconsidering making light of one of the darkest periods in European history, the Bard ditched the plague theme, changed the title, and composed the more "dreamy" tale with which we're familiar.

The Divorcing of the Harpy. Scholars still debate whether Shakespeare was forced into an arranged marriage after impregnating Anne Hathaway, eight years his senior, and if he was also involved with another woman at the time. An outline for this never-written comedy lays out the plot: A brilliant writer is held back by his unhappy wife and their "irksome brat spawn." Why did the Bard never move forward with this work? A note on the outline, in different handwriting than that of the author, reads, "If thou doth dare, I will reveal to all of London thou's troubles with drink, song, and further sordid merriment, in addition to the particularities of your nocturnal engagements with a certain Earl of Southampton."

The Oaf King of the Americas. This eerily prophetic, half-completed comedy tells of King George of Taysha, the foolish but impetuous leader of "a future land that lyeth across the seas." After his kingdom is attacked by a rogue group of knights from the East, George declares war. His advisor, the stern, war-minded "Richard Chain," was clearly a rough draft of Iago, the villain in *Othello*.

A Prince of Airs. This never-published sonnet recounts the tale of a young prince forced to relocate to another kingdom after he lands himself in "one minor clash and his mother became all affright." While it was never included in *The Complete Works of Shakespeare*, a mention of the sonnet in a late-1980s story published in the *Philadelphia Enquirer* about the "lost-works" dossier most likely inspired the development of the NBC sitcom *The Fresh Prince of Bel Air*.

NEW DEAL AGENCIES

When President Franklin D. Roosevelt sought to pull the country out of the Great Depression, he did so with the New Deal, the largest-ever (at the time) government spending initiative. Dozens of new government agencies were created, each handily referenced by an acronym, like the WPA (Works Progress Administration), SSA (Social Security Administration), and these.

DATEP (Department of American Transportation Efficiency Planning)

Originally conceived in 1933 as an organization that would oversee cross-continental roads projects, the head of the organization was a Chicagoan named Albert Fleming. The organization's focus was derailed by a preoccupation of Fleming's: assuring that commuters traveling on interstates had easy access to what he called "quick and hot food." The idea had been planted in his mind by his brother-in-law, Ray Kroc—who would go on to found McDonald's, which got cheap, no-bid lands on thousands of new highway off-ramps.

FOA (Federal Orphan Administration)

After "Fanny Mae" became the popular moniker for the Federal National Mortgage Association (FNMA), a *Washington Post* reporter in 1938 attempted to nickname the FOA the "Oliver Administration" after Oliver Twist, the Charles Dickens character. However, the FOA's demoralizing task of overseeing the growing ranks of orphanages was simply too tragic to garner the kind of media attention required to sustain a cute nickname.

OEEIAAS (Office of Emergency Employment Interview Assistance and Affairs and Seminars)

Promoted as an agency that would help the unemployed get back to work by providing job training and interview assistance, it was shut down in 1940 after a congressional inquiry found that its sole success had been in providing new hats, which it hopefully called "interview hats," to unemployed men.

AHSS (Agency for Home Seamstresses Skills)

Known colloquially as "the darn-it-all agency," the AHSS was largely responsible for the institution of "home economics" curriculum in schools across the country. Skills covered in home economics, such as darning socks, had previously been passed from mother to daughter, but with women entering the workforce during the war, there was widespread concern that young women would no longer learn these skills at home.

FCFP (Federal Circus and Carnival Project)

After moderate controversy spread through the Midwest in 1934 about mistreatment of circus animals, the FCFP was created. The group also issued certificates that assured patrons that the little people were, in fact, small adults that were legally allowed to work and not exploited children, as well as certifications of authenticity for both bearded and fat ladies.

FAST FOOD FLOPS

• Low-carb/high-protein dieting was the biggest weight-loss fad of the early 2000s. McDonald's jumped on the bandwagon with the Low-Carb McMeat Mac, tested in a few cities. It was set up like an original Big Mac, but instead of three slices of bun, diners got three slices of meat. And on top of that meat was the regular meat (and cheese slices) that came on a regular Big Mac, for a total of five beef patties. That was too much meat, apparently, as the item was discontinued after three months.

• Subway is best known for its healthy sandwiches of lean meats and vegetables. It still sells less-healthy sandwiches, such as meatball, chicken Parmesan, and, for six months in 2006, the Starcher—a double-decker sandwich (meaning three pieces of bread) stuffed with potato chips, Doritos, saltine crumbles, corn, pretzels, and a scoop each of pasta salad, potato salad, and three-bean salad. A foot-long Starcher had more than 500 grams of carbohydrates.

• Elvis Presley died in August 1977 of a heart attack due in part to his poor diet. In August 1997, the Orange Julius smoothie chain commemorated the King's death with a drink based on his favorite snack, the peanut butter, bacon, and banana sandwich. That's a smoothie made up of bananas, peanut butter, bacon bits, cream, and sugar syrup. Named the "Love Me Blender," it was reportedly Orange Julius's worst-selling drink of all time.

• Pizza Hut's Stuffed Crust Pizza, in which mozzarella cheese is baked into the crust, was the company's most successful product launch ever. In 1998 the chain took it up a notch by stuffing pizza into the crust of a pizza. Extra yeast was added in the outer pizza's crust, so it would puff up enough to create the extra room needed to shove in a calzone ring—a crusty pizza pocket filled with cheese, tomato sauce, pepperoni, and sausage. Pizza Hut called it the P-N-P, or "Pizza in a Pizza." However, the extra weight in the crust made it too difficult to eat, and the calzones often leaked out. It was discontinued in 2000.

• While KFC isn't the only chicken chain, it's the most successful one, and in 2002 executives reasoned it was because of the signature "11 herbs and spices" breading. That was the logic behind OutSides: bite-size, deep-fried balls of the chain's famous breading…with absolutely no chicken inside. Test-marketed in Denver, one of the nation's most physically fit cities, the breading balls did not catch on.

• Domino's Pizza serves an Oreo Dessert Pizza, with a chocolate crust topped by crushed Oreo cookies and icing. The item came about because of a bizarre request at a Domino's on the Rutgers University campus in 2004. Late one night, some college kids came in with a bag of Oreos and asked the staff to throw the cookies on a pizza and bake it. They did, and the news spread, with the Oreo Pizza becoming a savory-sweet phenomenon, first locally, and then on the Internet. There were so many requests for the Oreo Pizza that Domino's briefly added it to their nationwide menu.

UNICORN FACTS

• The *Historiae Animalium*, a text describing all the animals living on Earth, included a description of unicorns in its 1620 edition.

• Unlike the Western unicorn and South American unicorn, the Asian unicorn is multi-colored, rather than white, with a scaly body and a flesh-covered horn.

• Powder ground from the horns of European unicorns has long been used for its curative properties—it's been an ingredient in everything from over-the-counter pain relievers to teething gel for babies.

• Powder ground from the horn of the South American unicorn can have hallucinogenic properties; mind-altering mushrooms are a part of that unicorn's diet. Effects of ingestion of South American unicorn horn can include panic attacks, depression, and paranoid delusions.

• It's a myth that unicorns avoid eye contact with humans because people are "less than pure-hearted." Unicorns are actually farsighted, which means the closer a human comes to a unicorn, the fuzzier they appear to the animal, so unicorns look away or back up.

TWO BEATLES NEAR-REUNIONS

In February 1980, the four band members convened for the first time in a decade in a recording studio on George Harrison's Scotland estate to record a song for a Harrison solo album. Ringo Starr was learning studio production at the time (via a correspondence course), and in all the chaos of setting audio levels, he forgot to press "record." The mistake wasn't discovered until Lennon and McCartney had left. They were never able to schedule time to get back together, as McCartney was going on a world tour and Lennon was recording *Double Fantasy* in New York.

In 1977 *Saturday Night Live* producer Lorne Michaels famously went on the air and pleaded with the Beatles to reunite, offering them the comically low sum of $3,000. Amazingly, John Lennon and Paul McCartney, were watching the live show together in Lennon's apartment that night. They decided to head out to the show and accept the offer, but it was nearing midnight, and the NBC studio was more than 30 blocks away. So McCartney called the only person he knew in New York who would be still awake and had a car: Ringo Starr. The three Beatles (Harrison wasn't in town at the time...although he had hosted *SNL* just a week earlier) were all set then to reunite on national television...except they didn't, because Starr got lost on the way to Lennon's apartment...which was on the same street as Starr's townhouse.

ABANDONED RULES OF 19TH-CENTURY BASEBALL

• The batter could take his bat with him as he ran to first base, in order to knock away a ball thrown to the first baseman to tag him out…or to knock away the first baseman.

• Sliding was banned, because it was considered "ungentle-manly."

• The hitter was allowed 12 balls before a walk, but three foul balls equaled an out.

• If the player on first base could manage to safely run to the pitcher's mound before advancing to second base (or with a stop at the mound between second and third), an out was erased from his team's tally for the inning.

• The ball was much heavier back then (the "dead ball" era, because the ball was rarely hit out of the park, and usually thudded out in the infield). Result: The ball was seldom hit to left field. For that reason, it was written into the rules that both teams must man the area with a billygoat.

• Another player was stationed between first and second, much like the shortstop between second and third. He was called the "longstop."

• Mustaches were required for all players except pitchers. Pitchers were barred from having mustaches after the 1878 Youngstown Ballplayers pitching staff all grew extremely long handlebar mustaches that they would twirl in an effort to distract batters.

• Underhand pitching was permitted, but since pitchers who did it were booed and called sissies by opposing players, fans, and teammates, the practice died out.

• In the 1880s, the designated hitter was a separate position. Called a PAB, it was short for "primarily a batswain."

THE ORIGIN OF BRUNCH

In 1962 executive chef John Brunchman left his job of 10 years at New York's famous Waldorf-Astoria hotel to open up his own Manhattan restaurant, Brunchman. One of the things he hated about being a chef, however, was the terrible hours: He didn't like arriving at work at 4 a.m. on the weekends to prepare for the hotel's elaborate breakfast service. So when he opened Brunchman, he decided not to open until 10 a.m. But he still wanted to serve breakfast. He noticed that groups of people would come in at 10 and 11, and some would order breakfast items while others, since it was so close to midday, would order lunch. This gave Brunchman the idea to combine his breakfast and lunch menus into one and create a combination meal called "brunch," which, like the first restaurant that served it, he named after himself.

BRITISH SLANG

Crumble: Piece of cake

Frattle: Scuffle or argument

Puffy: Jacket

Leggies: Tights

Sockies: Feet

Bee: Short for rugby, Great Britain's second most popular sport after soccer

Splished: Drunk

Plaidsy: Derogatory word for a Scottish person

Knobly: Confused

Bismuthed: Feeling nauseated

A bit green and stuffed: To have a cold

Pink: One-pound note (they're pink)

Navy: Five-pound note (they're blue)

Hollow: Apartment

Benji: Wristwatch (because Big Ben is a large clock)

THE "VICE PRESIDENT FOR A DAY" PROGRAM

When you were a kid, were you ever named a "junior deputy" by a policeman visiting your school, and he gave you a neat police badge sticker? That's very similar to what President Martin Van Buren did when he was president (1837–41). He came from a large family and had 16 nieces and nephews, all of whom wanted to visit "Uncle Marty" in the White House. So once a month, one of the children would come to Washington and spend a day or two, following Van Buren around on official presidential business and participating in an Oval Office "swearing in" ceremony for the "Special Honorary Vice President for the Day." The tradition ended when Van Buren left office.

But when Harry Truman's approval ratings began to fall in 1951, just prior to his running for reelection, a staffer remembered reading about Van Buren's cute tradition and suggested to Truman that creating a "Vice President for a Day" program would be a great way to reward hardworking and civic-minded students while also boosting the president's image.

The program worked like this: Students across the country were nominated by a teacher, minister, or Scout leader on the basis of academic achievement or public service. Once a month, one lucky kid aged 12–17 would be flown to Washington, D.C., and shadow the president for a day. Many future political and cultural leaders were selected as "Vice President for a Day" during the program's 12-year life, including actor Clint Eastwood and future real vice president Gerald Ford. In all, more than 130 upstanding youths—male and female, of all races and religions—got to be vice president for a day.

The program came to a quiet, and permanent, end in 1981. In recognition for her work starting a food bank in her home-town of Van Nuys, California, 15-year-old Alison Perkley got to be Vice President for a Day on March 30, 1981…the day President Ronald Reagan was shot. Later in the day, actual VP George Bush stepped in to assume temporary control. But for about two hours, Bush was en route via airplane, and couldn't be reached. This meant that for that period of time, Perkley was the acting president of the United States, and she was even sworn in by the Chief Justice of the Supreme Court. She spent her brief presidential term in a White House office, watching for news about the attempted Reagan assassination on TV, and crying. The Vice President for a Day Program was quietly ended by Congress two weeks later.

BROADWAY ADAPTATION FLOPS

• *Star Wars* is probably the biggest pop culture phenomenon of all time. And it was more than just a billion-dollar box-office success: comic book, radio, and TV adaptations have all scored big. What didn't hit: a Broadway version. Staged in 1979, between the film releases of *Star Wars* and *The Empire Strikes Back*, producers of *Star Wars: The Musical* made the amazingly bad decision that since they couldn't compete with the special effects of the movie, they shouldn't, so they just put up big screens and projected battle scenes from the movie as actors ran around the stage in cardboard space-ships. (The music was written by John Williams, and lyrics were by pop star Leo Sayer.) George Lucas cancelled the show after a week, and then told the media it was supposed to be a "short engagement" to begin with. (Search YouTube for bootlegs: You'll want to hear the Princess Leia character sing a love ballad called "Familiar Lover," set to the tune of the *Star Wars* march, to Luke Skywalker.)

• After the Broadway success of two musicals based on his classic movies *The Producers* and *Young Frankenstein,* Mel Brooks went back to his own well. But lightning did not strike a third time, because he chose to adapt *Silent Movie*. It was a funny, well-received popular film, so why didn't it work as a musical? Because the original was innately about film, and it didn't make sense on stage. Broad facial gestures were difficult for the audience to make out while cast members ran around silently on stage as an orchestra played zany music.

Fun fact: The Oscar-winning movie *The Artist* was set to go into production as a play in Paris in 2009, until the failure of *Silent Movie* made the producers realize it would be better as a movie—a silent movie.

• *Aquaman: Turn Off the Wet* was staged in the grand performance area of SeaWorld in San Diego, where Shamu usually performs his tricks. A lot of the budget went to working out underwater acoustics, building a tank large enough to house a show, and hiring Cyndi Lauper to write the songs. At a final cost of $30 million, the show was cancelled after three weeks of filling stands at an average of 10 percent capacity. A move to the New York Public Aquarium was cancelled.

• Speaking of Oscar winners, *Rain Man* won Best Picture in 1989, and 10 years later it hit Broadway with a mixture of showy Vegas-style performance numbers, long driving sequences, and songs including "Gonna Make it Rain," "Counting Cards" and "Excellent Driver." It was immediately controversial and widely panned. Raymond, the main character, is autistic, and a dancing autistic man was deemed in bad taste by the Autism League, particularly the sequence in which he dreams of being able to "not be the rain man, but be a rain dance, dancer, man." Frank Rich summed it up in the *New York Times*: "Everybody hates *Rain Man*."

QUIRKY LAS VEGAS THEME HOTELS

The Allies

Nearly half of all visitors to Las Vegas are age 70 or over. The defining event of their generation was World War II, so Las Vegas's The Allies Hotel sought to tap into that age-group with its WWII-themed hotel. Visitors had a choice of three room styles: "Army Barracks," "Officers Quarters," or "Stalag 17." There were two dining areas: One served military-style cafeteria food while the other, The Ration Hall, doled out meager portions made from canned and packaged ingredients. Nightly entertainment included Bing Crosby, Bob Hope, and Andrews Sisters impersonators. The 1994 Visit Fabulous Las Vegas guide called The Allies "deeply depressing and in questionable taste." It closed in 1998.

Clark County Community College

The Clark County Community College Hotel and Resort sought to evoke the sense of a community or junior college. Why? The proprietors had had some luck converting old schools into brewpubs, and they thought that turning a college campus (this was once a real college, right off the Vegas strip) into a resort was the next logical step. It didn't work. Rooms were too small (they were dorm rooms), the "dining hall" and DVD "library" understocked, and staff was instructed to be cold, distant, and answer "I dunno" to any question. Many college advisors recommend that students attend community college for a while to save money and get some credits out of the way before transferring to a four-year college. This was echoed in the advertising for the CCCCH&R: "Going to Vegas? Spend the first half at the Clark County Community College Hotel and Resort, and save some money!"

The Tooth

Almost nobody likes going to the dentist, a fact lost on the consortium of wealthy California–based dentists who funded The Tooth Hotel and Casino in 2000. The resort had a dental theme—beds were shaped like dentists' chairs, "laughing gas" (really potpourri) was released from ceiling-mounted dispensers every 15 minutes, and only sugar-free desserts were sold in The Tooth's dining areas. The hotel's claim to fame was its annual World's Only Indoor Marathon, held in an adjacent arena—competitors ran 26.2 miles around a track, ostensibly a reference to the dental-horror movie *The Marathon Man*. The hotel remains open thanks to numerous dental-industry conventions.

The Las Vegas Experience

Two of Las Vegas's most popular hotels are New York, New York, which delivers a New York experience, and the Paris, which recreates Paris, down to romantic bistros and a mini-Eiffel Tower. Some developers thought that the market was ripe for a resort designed to re-create another of the world's greatest cities: Las Vegas. The Las Vegas Experience opened in Las Vegas in 2005 and featured exacting, miniature replicas of many of Las Vegas's most ionic attractions, such as a pirate ship like Treasure Island's, fountains like the Bellagio's, and, evoking the Paris, a mini-mini-Eiffel Tower.

FORGOTTEN FAD: NON-WORKING WATCHES

Most everybody has a cell phone these days, and their cell phones have clocks on them, which diminishes the need for wristwatches. In turn, watches have become the ultimate status symbol—the more expensive and gem-encrusted they are, the more wealthy folks want to show them off, even though they're kind of useless. Oddly enough, when wristwatches first gained mainstream popularity in the 1890s, they were also viewed as a useless (because there were clock towers throughout every city) but costly status symbol.

A popular fashion among the wealthy families and tycoons of New York just before the turn of the 20th century was to wear wristwatches that didn't even work—they couldn't be wound and the hands wouldn't move. The watches were cast in gold or silver and decorated with diamonds and other precious stones. A watch became a double status symbol: It showed off material wealth and implied that the person wearing it was so privileged that they didn't even need to use it to tell the time, or so "idle rich" that they didn't have any appointments anyway.

FACTS ABOUT THE 50 STATES

Alabama. The state's official rock n' roll song is the Lynyrd Skynyrd classic "That Smell."

Alaska. In 1991 the U.S. sold the territory to Canada for $42 million, or 10 cents an acre. Citizens born prior to that year enjoy dual citizenship.

Arizona. The Southwestern state gets more snowfall each year than Michigan.

Arkansas. Largest city: Little Rock (population 190,000). Smallest city: Big Rock (population: 242).

California. The large Western state had a population of only 30,000 until millions moved there in 1940, seeking the life described in John Steinbeck's novel *The Grapes of Wrath*.

Colorado. Official state tree: the blue spruce. Official state beverage: Pepsi.

Connecticut. So many people live in this state and commute for work into New York City that the city nearly annexed the entire state in 1992. The ballot measure failed, 51 to 49 percent.

Delaware. The tiny Northeastern state is technically still under the control of England. After the American Revolution, paperwork was drawn up to release the U.S. from British rule. Delaware's representatives never signed it.

Florida. A recent survey found that as many as 2.2 percent of Florida's residents can speak dolphin.

Georgia. "Georgia peach" is the local term for ham.

Hawaii. Up until 2004, the best way to get around the hundreds of tiny islands that make up the state was by boat or helicopter. Today: A high-speed gondola system connects all of the Hawaiian Islands.

Idaho. The first American concert played by the Beatles happened in a Boise, Idaho, concert hall in 1961. A dozen people showed up.

Illinois. Illinois nearly split into two states in 1974 when an especially corrupt Chicago mayor tried to create "Chicagoland" as a way to evade tax debts and criminal charges.

Indiana. The oldest continually inhabited place in North America.

Iowa. Official state bird: comedian (and native) Tom Arnold.

Kansas. Cable TV is paid for by the state, provided that it includes the Kansas Channel, a state-run news organization that airs what media watchdog groups have labeled "Midwestern propaganda."

Kentucky. A favorite local delicacy is Retired Racehorse Chili. (It's just a nickname. The chili often includes non-racing horses.)

Louisiana. Until 1920, it was a prison colony for pirates.

Maine. Wednesday is "Free Ice Cream Day" for all Mainers.

Maryland. A 1747 law requires everyone meeting on the street to address one another as "Mary."

Massachusetts. Over 80 percent of residents are at least partially a Kennedy.

Michigan. The northern state gets more 100-plus-degree days each year than Arizona.

Minnesota. The state is famous for its "10,000 lakes" and "Twin Cities," but in reality, Minnesota has just two lakes, but 10,000 cities.

Mississippi. In a 2011 statewide poll, Mississippians said their favorite state was Alabama.

Missouri. Franco is a suburb of Independence, Missouri, and, ironically, is also the name of a fascist Spanish dictator.

Montana. Named after the Spanish word for mountain, because the state's entire early population of Spanish settlers lived on a single mountaintop in the central region of the area.

BEHIND SUPER BOWL I

The Super Bowl was not always the near-national holiday of pomp, celebration, and media mania it is today. In the first years, the Super Bowl was extremely low-key. The game came about when the two professional, regional football leagues, the NFL (New England Foot Ball League) and the AFL (All-West Football League), merged into one. Here are some little-known facts about it.

• The Los Angeles Rams of the AFL faced off against the Cleveland Steamers of the NFL. Back then, football was more of a kicking game, not a passing and touchdown game. This is reflected in Super Bowl I's final score: 9 to 6, Los Angeles.

• All nine of the Rams' points were scored by kicker Don Simmons, who was named the game's Most Valuable Player. This is the only time a kicker would be a Super Bowl MVP.

• Today it's held at a giant stadium that's neutral to each of the two teams, and usually in a warm climate. In 1967 league organizers contacted the operators of 12 league-affiliated stadiums. All turned them down, so it was played on the football field at Cal State Fullerton.

• The first Super Bowl Sunday—December 23, 1967—was a Wednesday.

• Only 9,000 fans showed up.

• Food vendors didn't even bother to set up shop for the day. The only food available were individual-size boxes of Grape Nuts provided by the game's sponsor, Post.

• It wasn't televised, but it was available on the radio in only Los Angeles and Cleveland. A 15-minute recap show aired on NBC affiliates in a handful of cities (which included Los Angeles, but not Cleveland).

• Today, the post-Super Bowl spot on TV is used to launch new TV series or present special episodes of existing shows. Airing after the 15-minute recap was a made-for-TV movie version of *The Shoemaker and the Elves.*

• The halftime entertainment, today a spectacle centered around a major pop or rock star, was more restrained in 1967: The Fullerton Baptist Church Men's Choir sang Christmas carols.

• Pre-game entertainment included pop crooner Jack Jones singing the national anthem, a skit by the cast of *The Gary Moore Show*, and a Frisbee-throwing contest for children.

DINER LINGO

Neutered Joe

Decaf coffee that is kept in a regular pot (without the orange lid) and secretly served to jittery customers who will be even harder to deal with if they get more caffeine.

Aggro Joe

Regular coffee that is kept in a decaf pot—usually spiked with Red Bull energy drink—and secretly served to annoying customers who ask for decaf.

Surf-and-Turfers

A table full of office workers who are using company funds to pay for their meal. Waitstaff are trained to push the most expensive menu items on surf-and-turfers.

Hitchcocking

The act of the entire staff standing perfectly still while silently staring at patrons who have failed to leave even though the restaurant is obviously closing. Every 30 seconds or so, they take one step closer to the offenders.

iPutz

A patron who is more interested in texting than in giving the waiter their order.

Menu Degreaser

This low-level employee has to remove the grease and bits of the previous day's leftover food from menus.

EUI-ers

Short for "Eating Under the Influence." Refers to patrons who are obviously intoxicated.

Jack Attack

A patron who is overly concerned with the cleanliness of the table and silverware. Inspired by Jack Nicholson's obsessive-compulsive character in *As Good As It Gets*.

Pie in the Sky

Diner regulars who come in and only order a piece of pie and a cup of coffee so they can sit at the counter and flirt with the waitresses.

TLC Soup

Short for "Tastes Like Chicken." This soup is made from un-eaten food and aging mystery meat that missed the trash can. It's sprinkled with copious amounts of salt and pepper to mask the mop-water taste. Reserved for patrons who take several minutes to give their order, only to end up asking for the soup of the day.

DOT-COM BUSTS

Socks-Online.com

Buying clothes online seems kind of weird, but not socks—you don't really need to try them on before you buy (nor are you allowed to). Still, most people tend to buy socks immediately when they need them, not by logging on to the Internet to peruse, purchase, and wait for them. "The Internet's #1 destination for socks, and only socks" as Socks-Online billed itself, was a hard sell, even though it offered more than 50 styles of socks. The website shuttered in November 2000, shortly after it received a cease-and-desist letter from the White House because it used a cartoon rendering of Socks the Cat, President Bill Clinton's pet cat, as its mascot.

WebNewspaper.com

The Internet marked a major shift in how information is distributed and consumed: The world doesn't read as many newspapers as it used to; instead, we get most news from the Internet, albeit a lot of that is from newspapers' websites. WebNewspaper wanted to bridge that gap for new Internet users. It contracted with several newspapers, including *USA Today*, the *Charlotte Observer*, and the *San Francisco Chronicle* to allow customers (who paid a monthly fee of $29.99) to visit their website and print out the newspaper. WebNewspaper did not allow visitors to read the news on their screens—articles had to be printed out. After it attracted fewer than 400 subscribers, the site went dark.

HomeLaundry.com

Grocery shopping and delivery websites like Webvan and HomeGrocer died quick deaths, and so did this online service that asked customers to outsource another hated task of household drudgery: laundry. The site had a lot of problems, the first of which was its extremely high prices: $20 per load of laundry, plus extra for soap and water (and even more for warm or hot water), and $10 a load for drying. And the service wouldn't accept underwear or towels. The site was also besieged with unhappy customers. HomeLaundry promised a 24-hour turnaround, but the wait time was far longer: an average of five days in the San Francisco area. If customers did get their clothes returned, they were damaged or ruined. HomeLaundry opened and closed in 1999.

Frizzlgyrztk.com

Lots of websites have funny names: Google, Yahoo!, or Bing, for example. But none is as odd—or as hard to pronounce—as Frizzlgyrztk. But the most peculiar thing about the website is what service or product it offered. A visit yielded little more than stock photos of people happily looking at computers, accompanied by page after page of copy about "a portal to optimizing your e-commerce web solutions, right here on the Internet." When the company launched its IPO in July 1999, a reporter for *The New Republic* uncovered evidence that the site was an elaborate scam operated by a Chechen rebel organization. Within hours of the story being published, Frizzlgyrztk closed down.

RANDOM BITS OF KNOWLEDGE

• The most popular dog in Ireland is the Afghan Hound; the most popular dog in Afghanistan is the Irish Wolfhound.

• Red Bull contains no caffeine. The active ingredient is a weak cousin of lithium.

• In 1972 math was replaced in Rhode Island schools with industrial-arts education, at the request of the governor, who owned a large welding company.

• Children choke on green Gummi Bears more than on any other food.

• Starbucks has trademarked the shade of green it uses in its stores and employee uniforms.

• Just 100,000 Segways have ever been sold—more than half to the oil-rich nation of Yemen, where they are used by the military.

• Television was invented, and widely in use in Europe, before radio.

DISCARDED BAND NAMES

• Before they settled on "the Beatles" in 1959, the Fab Four tried out several other band names, including the Beas, the Ceaterpillars, the Greashoppers, the Eants, the Leadybugs, the Ceantipedes, and the Rolling Stones.

• The members of the Who suggested, and rejected, the What, the When, the Why, the Where, and the How.

• They ultimately were the Sex Pistols, but they could have been the Fornication Squirt Guns or the Nooky Rifles.

• Pink Floyd was almost named Beige Meat. (They used the name as an alias when checking into hotels on concert tours.)

• When Coldplay lead singer Chris Martin was filling in the blanks on his first record contract in 1997, he accidentally transposed two letters, thus legally negating his band's original name, Clodplay.

• In 2005, 18-year-old Kesha Rose Sebert sent an audition tape to MTV in the hopes of landing a role on P. Diddy's reality show, *Making the Band*. But the 's" key on Sebert's keyboard didn't work; she could only type her name as "Ke$ha."

TWIN FACTS

• Twins are well known to talk to one another in their own secret language. Linguists have studied this phenomenon, and, amazingly, the twin language is almost always extremely similar to a Belgian dialect of French. It's this dialect 95 percent of the time, researchers say, regardless of the twins' birthplace or heritage.

• Most octuplets are technically four sets of twins—four eggs are each implanted separately and then all split in two.

• The only conjoined (or "Siamese") twin to hold elected office in the U.S. was Oregon senator Mark Hatfield, who served from 1967 to 1997. While Hatfield became one of the most respected statesmen of his generation, his conjoined twin brother, Gary Hatfield, was a convicted white-collar criminal and was not allowed inside the Senate chamber. This required Hatfield to sit as close to the door as possible, while Gary sat just outside the door, with headphones on while the Senate was in session. It wasn't well known that Sen. Hatfield was a conjoined twin until after his death in 2011. Thought to be a political liability, Gary was an open secret among the press corps, who made great pains never to photograph Mark and Gary together, even during campaign stops and when Mark Hatfield threw out the first pitch at a Washington Senators game in 1970. Today, Gary Hatfield lives quietly in a suburb of Portland, Oregon.

• Twins are more likely to join the military, declare bankruptcy, be allergic to tomatoes, drop out of graduate school, get their pilot license, and be cremated than singles or triplets.

• Compared to singles, twins are far less likely to become farmers, garbage workers, or advertising executives, and also to give birth to twins, but far more likely to give birth to triplets. However, twins are less likely to marry than single-births.

ROADSIDE ATTRACTIONS

The Cob Farm

Just a few miles off Interstate 80 near York, Nebraska, the Harby family maintains the Cob Farm. The property is located on a 25-acre plot of land that's also used to grow corn. In 1963, in a barn on the Harby plot, Gerald Harby built a scale replica of the Nebraska State Capitol entirely out of corn cobs, varnish, and 2-by-4s. The family admits the name of the attraction does little to indicate the splendor of the 15-foot-high replica held within the barn, which itself could use a fresh coat of paint. "I ain't been to Lincoln to the see original yet," said Scott Harby, who operates the Cob Farm. "But judging by pictures, granddad did a fine job on it." Admission: $1.50.

Uncle Dave's Taxidermy Playland

One Yelp.com reviewer described this defunct schoolhouse-cum-taxidermy exposition outside of Great Falls, Montana, as "nightmarish." That's pretty accurate, as the exhibit is a schoolhouse, playground, and miniature Old West town populated entirely by taxidermied animals. The animals range from domestic (cat students propped up in desks in front of a cow teacher) to exotic (a cougar and a lion playing on the seesaw). Admission: free.

The American Bell-Bottom Museum

After marrying a teacher in 1980 and retiring from her modeling career, Judy Bertram (née Scott) was looking for a way to occupy her time. A longtime friend of English model Pattie Boyd, former wife of both Beatle George Harrison and Eric Clapton, Bertram said she was "struck in a dream one winsome evening" with a vision for creating a museum dedicated to the style of the era during which she saw her friend's biggest success. The museum itself (off Highway 101, near Hamilton, California) comprises nearly 200 mannequins, foam torso and leg forms, and clipped hangers, all outfitted in bell-bottoms, largely owned and worn by Bertram in the 1960s ad '70s. The highlight of the museum: a pair of denim bell bottoms Bertram claims were not only owned by Pattie Boyd, but were the inspiration for Clapton's 1971 song "Bell Bottom Blues." Admission: free, with a suggested donation of $5.

The World's Smallest Cobbler Shoppe

Opened by Percy Norwood in the 1970s in the sleepy, tiny town of Allegheny, Vermont, the World's Smallest Cobbler Shoppe is first notable for its custom-made door, which stands 4'6" high. The red door opens to a four-by-eight-foot retail area in which every surface, and three walls entirely covered with wooden cubby holes, are filled with vintage and antique shoes. While the store is small, the "world's smallest" designation does not refer to the shop itself, but the original cobbler/proprietor, Mr. Norwood, who stood 4'3". Mr. Norwood died before having the chance to confirm his "world's smallest cobbler" reputation with Guinness, but his son, Perry Norwood (5'9") continues to operate the shop in his honor. The shop itself is an operational cobbler/shoe repair shop, but tourists also like to pose outside the shop with the life-size plywood cutout of the elder Norwood. Admission: free.

GAFFES THAT ENDED PRESIDENTIAL CAMPAIGNS

Thomas Dewey, 1948

In 1948 Republican candidate Dewey was extremely confident that he would win the presidency over incumbent Harry Truman. He even went on a radio news show and said that he "guaranteed a win," and went on to make the assertion that he would "eat Harry Truman's heart on the National Mall." While Dewey led in the polls up to that point, Truman won in a landslide—millions of Americans didn't realize Dewey was joking.

Richard Nixon, 1960

In 1960 presidential debates were shown on television for the first time. Candidate John F. Kennedy came across as confident and self-assured; Nixon seemed nervous and shifty. Afterwards, Nixon sarcastically remarked to a reporter, "Kennedy's so handsome, I'd vote for him." What he meant was that handsomeness shouldn't be a replacement for political experience—it was an indictment of television as a news-carrying medium. Instead, Nixon appeared to be endorsing Kennedy... who won the election.

Barry Goldwater, 1964

On his only trip to the out-of-the-way city of Anchorage, Alaska, during his campaign, Goldwater left his microphone after a campaign rally. Backstage, supporters heard Goldwater remark to an aide that Alaska was "Canada's armpit" and "Let's get the heck away from these moose-jockeys." The

Republican Goldwater should have easily won the heavily Republican state, but for the first and only time, Alaska voted Democratic. Goldwater lost the election to Lyndon Johnson by only four electoral votes—which is how many Alaska had.

Gary Hart, 1988

In a stump speech in North Carolina during his campaign, Democratic candidate Gary Hart claimed to be so upstanding that he challenged anyone to find any dirt on him. Two days later, Hart was profiled on an episode of *60 Minutes*. A camera crew had followed Hart for a week, shooting footage of him walking around a crowded shopping mall, kissing a 19-year-old campaign staffer and remarking, "You smooch better than my wife."

H. Ross Perot, 1992

The third-party candidate alienated voters when he dropped out of and then reentered the presidential race. He actually exited and entered the contest eight times in four months. Perot ultimately earned 11 percent of the national popular vote, despite quitting the campaign three weeks before Election Day.

Paul Tsongas, 1992

Advisors warned primary candidate Tsongas that his difficult-to-pronounce name might hinder his campaign (his name is pronounced "song-gus"), but he paid them no mind. Instead, he played it up, utilizing the campaign slogan "Tsing a Tsong for Tsongas!" He was tsoundly defeated by Bill Clinton.

UNBUILT DISNEY THEME PARK ATTRACTIONS

Old Yeller Shootin' Gallery (1962)

Looking for an attraction to further spruce up Disneyland's Main Street, Walt Disney himself proposed this "dark ride" based on the infamous family film that traumatized a generation. At the attraction's conclusion, guests would have been allowed to use on-board BB guns to put a robotic version of the "rabid" pooch out of his misery. The idea didn't make it, mostly because of logistics—Disney feared that kids might shoot each other instead.

Bald Mountain Railroad (1975)

An early proposal for what eventually became the Big Thunder Mountain Railroad attraction in Disneyland, this roller coaster would have catapulted guests through a nightmarish wonderland straight out of the finale of *Fantasia*. Disney's Imagineers drew up concept sketches for scenes that included a graveyard with swirling ghost effects and a cavern featuring a 20-foot-tall animatronic "Chernabog" demon. The plans were scrapped, not because they were too scary, but because the coaster wouldn't mesh with the Wild West-themed Frontierland.

Hello Kitty of the Caribbean (1983)

When Disney began planning Tokyo Disneyland in 1983, it hoped to transplant its popular Pirates of the Caribbean ride. Unfortunately, very few people in Japan at the time were familiar with piracy or the legends surrounding them. Imagineers came up with a solution: Replace the pirates with Hello Kitty, the popular Japanese cartoon feline. Disney's design team cobbled together revised scenes for the attraction, which would have included an area where Hello Kitty tosses candy (in place of the original's cannonball attack) and another where the character hosts a costume contest instead of a "wench auction." The ride's theme song "Yo Ho (A Pirate's Life for Me)" became "It's a Fuzzy Wuzzy Life for Me." Workers were ready to break ground when someone pointed out a crucial flaw in the concept: The main character has no mouth, therefore unable to sing. The ride was scrapped.

Commander Starr: Battle for the Cherry Moon (1987)

Hot on the heels of *Captain EO*, a 3D short film featuring Michael Jackson that was a hit in Disneyland's Tomorrowland section, Disney executives were eager to come up with a similar project for the Epcot theme park in Orlando. They quickly made a deal for a film starring Prince, with Ridley Scott directing. Had the project taken off, Prince would have appeared as "Commander Starr," a character loosely based on Jamie Starr, one of his many pseudonyms in the '80s. Along with a group of futuristic revolutionaries played by Sheila E., Vanity, and the musician's other female protégés, Prince's character would have battled the forces of NOPE (New Order Power Empire), a fascistic, music-hating government in the far-off, post-apocalyptic year of 1999. Archived storyboards reveal a scene in which Commander Starr breaks out a phallic guitar gun and blasts stormtroopers with "nuclear funk rays" while riding atop a purple hovercraft on the moon. Plans were cancelled when execs realized it would be much cheaper to open a *Captain EO* attraction in Florida instead.

Americaland (1994)

Desperate to drive up attendance numbers at the company's fledgling Euro Disney theme park outside of Paris, then-CEO Michael Eisner reportedly came up with this idea during a limo ride through lower Manhattan. This new area, loosely modeled on Times Square, would have included an *Oliver and Company*-themed roller coaster, "All-American" hot-dog stands, and a haunted subway attraction featuring animatronic alligators and sewer creatures. When concept drawings were leaked to the French press, a poll showed that 48 percent of the nation's citizens said they'd sign a petition vowing never to set foot in the theme park.

The *Clerks* Quick Stop Shop (2000)

While scrounging for ways to help make Disney's MGM Studios "hipper" for 20-something guests, Imagineers came up with a concept for this elaborate merchandise shop in the park's "Streets of America" section. The interior and exterior would have been modeled on the Quick Stop, the New Jersey convenience store featured in director Kevin Smith's 1994 indie film *Clerks* (produced by the Disney-owned Miramax). Along with an array of merchandise based on other movies also released by Miramax, the staff would have been allowed to insult shoppers and spit on them, just like the characters in Smith's film. The suits at Disney balked at this edgy idea, and at proposed merchandise that would have included replicas of Samuel L. Jackson's "badass" wallet from *Pulp Fiction*, *The Crow* makeup kits, *Swingers*-branded martini shakers, and *Good Will Hunting* "math fun books."

LITERARY SEQUELS

Scout Finch and the Mystery of the White Hood

Harper Lee wrote *To Kill a Mockingbird* (1960), one of the most widely read and powerful novels of the 20th century… but that's the only book she ever published. She's extremely private and only occasionally speaks at an event or writes an article. She had no interest and saw no point in a sequel when offered more than $4 million by Random House in 1965 to write one…so they hired a ghostwriter (for far less than Lee–$2,500) named Tom Dixon, a prolific hack who had written more than 40 Nancy Drew books in the 1940s and '50s. Writing under the name Lee Harper, Dixon wrote a tale that mixed the characters and anti-racism of the original *Mockingbird* with the predictable sleuthing of Nancy Drew. In *Scout Finch and the Mystery of the White Hood*, plucky nine-year-old Scout Finch uncovers a secret Ku Klux Klan–like organization, exposes them, and gets them arrested, earning her a "junior deputy" badge from the local police department. The book was released to a flurry of press, but was critically lambasted and sold just 5,000 copies. Random House cancelled a planned line of Scout Finch mystery novels.

The Jovian Plague

Leo Tolstoy wrote a sequel to *War and Peace*, his sprawling 1869 epic about the French invasion of Russia, in 1909, just a year before he died. He was very ill with pneumonia, however, and dictated much of his final novel, *The Jovian Plague*, to his nurse/secretary, who was barely literate. Not helping matters was Tolstoy's inconsistent consciousness and addiction to morphine. The novel is a rehash of *War and Peace*, except that it takes place in outer space, of which little was known at the time. It's set on Mars instead of in Russia, and the stand-ins for the invaders from France are "space lizards from Jupiter."

Back to the Farm

The Soviet Union eventually crumbled and abandoned Communism in 1991...50 years after George Orwell predicted it would in *Back to the Farm*, his prescient sequel to *Animal Farm*, his 1945 all-animal Communism satire. In *Back to the Farm*, the animals that converted to socialist ways slowly ease up on their political dogma and allow in the fun, free influences of a reportedly wonderful farm somewhere in the West. At the end, the animals embrace democratic principles (although corrupt ones), just so they can have access to extra-delicious feed without waiting in line for days to procure it.

Lonnie

In 1976, six years after he wrote *Deliverance*, author James Dickey published *Lonnie*, a novel focusing on the breakout character of the book (and the 1972 film adaptation): Lonnie, the banjo-playing inbred boy. Inspired by his favorite novel, James Joyce's difficult, stream-of-consciousness *Finnegans Wake*, Dickey wrote Lonnie as a series of monologues, off the top of his head, over a three-day weekend, and in an impenetrable Southern dialect (example: "Ah bun libin on dis buyoo fuh plum on fideen errs"). As Lonnie truly communicates through his banjo, Dickey intersperses the character's long soliloquies with bluegrass music, rendered in the book as dizzying, rapid-fire banjo tablature.

The Fury and the Führer

John Steinbeck realized that he'd had a lot of anger as a younger man, and it had manifested in two of his most memorable characters: Tom Joad, the angry migrant laborer from *The Grapes of Wrath*, and George, the angry migrant laborer from *Of Mice and Men*. As a way to reconcile both his own unresolved rage at the world, and that of his characters, Steinbeck wrote a novel in which Tom and George meet at a labor rally, then team up to find and murder ex-Nazi war criminals in 1949 Argentina. It ends with Hitler strangling Tom and George with one hand around each of their throats, until Hitler is squeezed to death by an unexpected guest: the ghost of George's old *Of Mice and Men* partner, Lennie. Steinbeck couldn't get the novel, tentatively titled *The Fury and the Führer*, published because it was, in the words of one editor, "horrible."

Finnegans Wake: Episode II

James Joyce's *Finnegans Wake* (1939) is famous because it's an impenetrable story written in stream-of-consciousness. Experts say the book is a comic novel about the Earwicker family. It's not—it's the first book of a planned science-fiction trilogy. Joyce finished the second part weeks before his death in 1941, which further detailed the people of Planet Earwick in their fight against octopus-like space pirates for galactic dominance. *Episode III* was never written.

PIRATE ORIGINS

Parrots

According to the Pirate Code, pirates believed that when pirates were killed or otherwise died at sea, their souls fled their bodies and stole the fleshy vessel of the closest non-human living creature. Parrots were often found in the tropical or island locales frequented by pirates, and many pirates believed that their fallen mates took up the bodies of the colorful birds. Pirates started toting parrots around with them to keep their "friends" around.

Burying treasure
Postmortem forensic testing on the remains of known pirates has revealed a high prevalence of obsessive compulsive disorder. Scientists and sociologists believe that the bizarre need for pirates to bury their treasure deep underground is a manifestation of this powerful mental condition.

Eye patches
Up until the 1800s, criminals in the British Empire could only be arrested via an eyewitness if the witness could identity both of the pirate's eyes. To cut down on the chance that they would be identified, pirates took to wearing eyepatches as a legal loophole.

"Shiver me timbers!"
Protein sources were hard to come by on the high seas… except in the Caribbean, historically teeming with pirates and also with goat meat, a popular food in the predominantly French-speaking region. The phrase is a corruption of the French "Chevre, mes frères," which a pirate would call out to the rest of his crew when he plundered or found goat meat. It means, "Goat, my brothers!"

Colorful nicknames
Pirate crews were a tight-knit bunch and gave each other inside-joke nicknames, as friends do. Almost all nicknames from the golden age of piracy were meant to be ironic or silly. For example, the notorious Blackbeard was a redhead, and Redbeard was a blonde.

MYTHICAL REGIONAL MONSTERS

Wisconsin Grandma Hordes

An old farmers' tale says that there's a coven of old witches who emerge from the netherworld in late summer and hide deep in the cornfields of central Nebraska. Although the legend's popularity peaked in the 1970s, a few sightings of rogue "Grandmas" (so named because the horde is harmless, and the populace has grown affectionate toward their local legend) are still reported each year. They're usually dismissed as leaning corn stalks and creepy shadows seen by people who wander too far into a cornfield. The locals aren't taking any chances, however, and each September several small Nebraska towns put on "Grandma Fests" in which the "Grand Children" (kids dressed up as old people) throw rolling pins and fake flowers into cornfields as they ask the Wisconsin Grandma Hordes not to spoil the harvest.

Worcester Tornado

Rumors of a sentient twister have dogged residents of Massachusetts for more than a century. The most famous survivor account came from Worcester native Henry "Hank" Plank in 1887. "We was all in the cellar hiding from the twister," Plank told the *Boston Globe*. "I looked out the winder and saw her [the tornado] jump right over top of our pig house. Then I yelled, 'Ha! You missed, you dumb tornado!' Then she stopped right in her path and turned back around and she leveled that old pig house. And then as she twirled away she shook her hips back and forth like she was laughing at me! That thing was alive as sure as I'm standing here talking to you." Similar stories of a "twister with an attitude" have led locals to believe that it's either one intelligent tornado that keeps getting re-born, or perhaps a race of godlike tornados.

Eskimopie

In the early 20th century, white settlers in the upper Yukon were concerned that their children might get "savaged up" if they befriended children from the native tribes. To keep their kids close, the settlers told tall tales of delicious pies made from hard chocolate and vanilla ice cream, along with the frozen monster Eskimopie—the same size, shape, and color of a polar bear—that will "steal your desserts forever if you misbehave." We get the words Eskimo and Eskimo Pie from this legend.

Flaming Pink Guy

The legend of the Flaming Pink Guy can be traced back to school lunchrooms in southern Florida in 1978. Students, misunderstanding the warnings they'd heard at home, would tell their friends to stay off the streets at night because of "the Flaming Pink Guy," a creature seemingly made of glowing pink flames who would kidnap and consume his victims in hellfire. Parents were actually warning of "flaming pink eye," a condi-tion that was rampant in Florida nightclubs in the fall of 1978.

ITALIAN ESPRESSO DRINKS

Starbucks and other American coffee chains base their menus of lattes and mochas on traditional Italian coffeehouses, which devised a number of ways to serve coffee and milk—*con panna* is coffee with whipped cream, for example. Here are some other Italian favorites.

Canadiano: Like an Americano, but the barista writes down the name of the drink on the cup in both French and English and it costs about 10 percent more.

Caffe con arachide: Espresso poured over peanuts.

Caffé evaporato: Super-strong coffee made by making a strong espresso shot, then letting it sit for several days to let the water evaporate. This then condenses into a thick, incredibly bitter syrup. Baristas then mix the syrup with a fresh shot of hot espresso and a spoonful of honey.

Caffé con sugo salsiccia: Coffee with sausage gravy.

Caffé oleo: Italy experienced frequent shortages in the early 20th century, and used butter instead of milk in coffee. During World War II, butter was in short supply, too, so Italians started using margarine, also called oleo, in their coffee.

RARELY USED BUT LEGITIMATE CHESS RULES

• The queen can move wherever she wants, whenever she wants.

• The bishops may switch places, but only if they are in their original starting positions.

• It's okay to call a rook a "castle," but if you do, you forfeit a turn.

• Knights may not cross each other's path.

• You may not move the king until the game has been going for at least 10 minutes.

• Pawns may move backward, but only if there are no opposing pieces within a seven-spot radius.

• It's only enforced at the highest levels of professional play, but it is customary to move pieces with the left hand. If the player is left-handed, they must use their right hand.

• In non-Christian countries, the bishop is to be referred to as a "senator."

PREDICTIONS THAT DIDN'T COME TRUE

"This blasted thing will never catch on. These stupid teeth keep getting stuck. And it can't compete with the button."

—Gideon Sundbäck, inventor of the zipper, 1914

"This will be the first championship of many, the beginning of a veritable dynasty."

—James Hart, Chicago Cubs owner, after his team won the 1908 World Series

"I can't imagine anyone would feel comfortable operating a telephone while walking."

—Randall Thomas, AT&T president, rejecting a pitch for cellular phones, 1982

"Sorry, boys, but pop trios with an occupational band name and a lead singer whose one-word moniker can be used as both a noun and a verb never go anywhere."

—Edward West, Vice-President of Warner Bros. Records, on declining to sign the Police to a contract in 1975

"At least my old friend Brutus can be trusted."

—Julius Caesar, March, 44 B.C.

GOOGLE'S EASTER EGGS

In computer jargon, "Easter eggs" are little programmer jokes embedded in computer games, DVD menus, and even websites, particularly Google. For example, if you type "anagram" into the Google search field, it replies, "did you mean 'nag a ram'?" "Nag a ram" is, of course, an anagram for "anagram"! Here are some other Google tricks:

• If you type in "domo arigato," it replies "Mister Roboto."

• If you type in "Captain Kirk is the best," it returns photos of Captain Picard.

• If you type in "fake moon landing," it returns pictures of bananas.

• Googling images of Bill Paxton brings back images of Bill Pullman.

• Googling images of Bill Pullman returns images of Liam Neeson.

• Searching for "bacon recipes" brings back contact information for hospitals in your area.

MOON TRIVIA

• Around 4500 B.C., Sumerians thought the sun was a vain god who gazed all day at his own image. At night he used a mirror (the moon) to watch himself sleep.

• Because of a gravitational effect called "tidal coupling," the same side of the moon is always facing Earth. Not knowing this, Christopher Columbus predicted that he would sail far enough from Europe that he would be able to see a different side of the moon.

• Two-thousand years ago, the Moche people of western Peru believed that the moon was about 40% oxygen, 20% silicon, 20% magnesium, 10% iron, 3% each of calcium and aluminum, with trace amounts of chromium, titanium, and man-ganese. No one knows how they arrived at those numbers, but in the early 1970s NASA's moon missions found out the Moche were exactly right.

• Aristotle thought the moon was the lost island of Atlantis, banished to space by Zeus after Atlanteans dared to attack Athens.

• Immediately after leaving his footprint on the moon, astronaut Neil Armstrong tripped and fell on his face. The imprint from his helmet is still on the moon's surface.

TEEN IDOLS: WHERE ARE THEY NOW?

Jonathan Taylor Thomas, a teen idol in the early '90s from his role on TV's *Home Improvement*, graduated from USC's prestigious film school with honors in 2001. After that, he bummed around Europe, settling in Latvia, which he calls "the most beautiful country in the world." He's since become a major player in the burgeoning Latvian film industry, writing and directing four dark character studies, winning a total of five Stelvlaſ Awards, the Latvian equivalent of an Oscar. He's regarded as "the Orson Welles of Latvia."

Amy Carter, the outspoken, politically active daughter of President Jimmy Carter, secretly married Kevin Mondale, son of Carter's vice president, Walter Mondale. Carter–Mondale runs a nonprofit animal preservation charity in Maine.

El DeBarge and **Chico DeBarge** of the '80s pop group DeBarge pooled their fortunes to open up a series of restaurants housed on riverboats. They teamed up with the Midwestern Mexican food chain El Chico, and in 1995 opened El and Chico DeBarge's El Chico Barge.

At age 18, **Lance Kerwin** (*James at 16*) became a TV writer. He wrote for *Emergency!*, *Cagney and Lacey*, and *Scarecrow and Mrs. King*, along with several unsuccessful pilots, including *Police Man* and *Underwater White House: 2225*. He is now the head writer for the TNT series *Rizzoli and Isles*.

THE FIRST FOOD PYRAMID (1950)

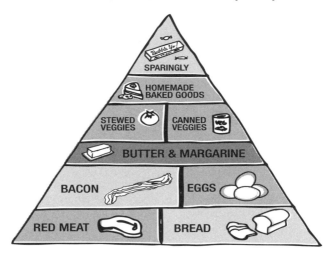

- Sparingly: bubblegum, licorice whips, penny candy

- 1–2 servings of homemade cakes and pies

- 2–3 servings of stewed green vegetables, cooked thoroughly to bring the nutrients to the surface

- 2–3 servings of canned vegetables and fruits, such as peaches in heavy syrup

- 8 servings of butter, margarine, or lard

- 4–5 servings of bacon

- 4 eggs (6 for "growing boys and girls")

- 7–9 daily portions of protein: ground beef, top sirloin, roundsteak

- 7–9 daily portions of grains: Wonder Bread, homemade bread, oatmeal

INTERESTING ANAGRAMS

"COOL TYPEWRITER" is an anagram for "MY COMPUTER."

"ELIZABETH, MONARCH OF BRITAIN" is an anagram for "GIVE UP IRELAND AND WALES."

"GEORGE JETSON, FUTURE MAN" is an anagram for "FRED FLINTSTONE REBOOT."

"BRAND NEW SPORTS CAR" is an anagram for "BIG DEBT MACHINE."

"UNICORN HORN" is an anagram for "UNREAL HORSE."

"FRED S. MACMURRAY" is an anagram for "MY THREE SONS."

"WENDY'S HAMBURGERS" is an anagram for "MCDONALDS CLONE"

"NANCY KERRIGAN'S KNEECAP" is an anagram for "TANYA HARDING IS GUILTY."

UNUSUAL WEATHER PHENOMENA

Sand hail

Clouds are made from moisture absorbed from the surface and waterways of the Earth. On the rare occasion when freezing temperatures occur in coastal areas, sand can evaporate into the sky and form clouds, which then puts that sand right back onto the earth in the form of "sand hail," falling grains of sand, encased in frozen water.

Hurricant

Hurricanes that touch down and destroy property always make the news, but those make up only 5 percent of all hurricanes observed. The remaining 95 percent are "hurricants," which are hurricanes that never touch down, instead hovering ominously over a fixed point for as long as three days.

Silent thunder

If there's lightning, then thunder usually precedes or follows it. Sometimes that thunder is so loud or so high-pitched that it's inaudible to human ears. Dogs, however, can hear it, and it hurts their ears, so if you see lightning but don't hear thunder, make sure to comfort your dog.

Invisible lightning

As stated, thunder and lightning go together. The sound

of thunder is noticeable, but the sight of lightning may be blocked by clouds. Or the lightning didn't come at all. If barometric pressure is high, thunder may sound and lightning may crash, but inconsistencies in the atmosphere render the lightning invisible to the human eye.

Frozen snow

Snow is very light, and so falls to the earth slowly and softly. If the conditions are cold enough for snow, they are also cold enough for chilling, winter winds. If the temperature falls below freezing and precipitation results in snow, and a system brings in winds, the winds themselves are freezing, which when meeting a snowfall, freezes the snow, mid-air.

Pink lightning

There's that old folk logic that says that a pink, calm sky at night portends a sunny tomorrow. It's mostly true, but if barometric pressure drops, a rainstorm can still happen during a pink sky at night, even with minimal clouds. This leads to warm rain, and because of the pink light filling the sky, the lightning actually looks pink.

Half rain

A combination of a light, quickly falling rain mixed with wind flowing upward results in half rain, in which rain falls…but never touches the ground, because it evaporates before it hits.

STRANGE JAPANESE VIDEO GAMES
NEVER RELEASED IN THE UNITED STATES

Mecha-Lizard vs. American Father (1981)

This arcade game was reminiscent of *Space Invaders* and starred a robotic reptile trying to fend off an army of Uncle Sam ("American Father") clones. His only weapon against the brigade's red lasers and cheeseburger bombs: his fire breath. Despite botching Sam's name, the title spawned a sequel two years later: *Ms. Mecha-Lizard vs. American Mother*, which featured a female reptile with a pink bow on her head facing an onslaught of machine-gun-toting blonde women in red, white, and blue bikinis.

Super Kool Kawaii Kangaroo (1983)

Despite an incredibly cute hero, the Kawaii Kangaroo, and graphics considered advanced for the era, the Australia-themed game was quickly pulled off the market. After players completed each level, the kangaroo performed a victory dance along with an all-koala chorus line in front of a flashing neon background. It caused almost instantaneous seizures in epileptics and certain dog breeds. A slew of lawsuits led the development company, Shigeru Games, to declare bankruptcy in early 1985.

Pinch! Every! Posterior! (1989)

Arcade games in Japan are often geared toward a mature

audience (arcades are often adults-only). This adults-only title included a unique glove controller that enabled players to "pinch" the behinds of on-screen women in levels with names like "Booty Beach" and "Tushy Tea House." Immensely popular, the game inspired tournaments in Kyoto and four sequels for both arcades and home consoles, including a version geared towards women called *Crotch Soccer Advanced*, featuring a boot controller that attached to players' feet.

Squid Snatcher (1995)

Claw machines are commonplace throughout Japan. But instead of Hello Kitty dolls or stuffed Sonic the Hedgehogs, the prizes up for grabs in these contraptions were live mollusks. Beset by numerous logistical problems, which included players getting squirted in the eye by squid ink, only a few were ever installed in arcades.

Salary Man (2003)

This *Sims*-like game, initially released for home computers, allows fans to relax after a hard day at the office by...working at an office. After designing a character and dressing him in one of 50 almost identical business suits, players are confronted with challenges like processing paperwork, in real time, for four hours while enduring barbs from an over-demanding boss. Despite the unappealing theme, the game and its numerous sequels, with titles like *Salary Man: Pets* and *Salary Man: Working for Vacation*, have collectively sold over 35 million copies.

ALMOST-USED NAMES FOR NBA TEAMS

• The New Jersey Nets originated in New York in 1972 under the ownership of the publishing group that ran the *New York Daily News,* who wanted to call the team the News. But not because of the paper—it was meant to refer to Frank Sinatra's song "New York, New York," with its famous first line, "Start spreading the news." Owners changed their minds at the last minute and went with Nets, because it rhymes with the names of the other local sports teams the Mets and the Jets.

• In 2005 the Utah Jazz, Los Angeles Lakers, and New Orleans Hornets entered into talks to "realign" their names. As is, they don't make sense: There isn't much jazz in Utah, there aren't any lakes in L.A. (the team originated in Minnesota, "land of 10,000 lakes"), and hornets aren't native to New Orleans (but they are to Charlotte, the team's original home). Owners of the three teams agreed to switch names around to result in the Utah Lakers (Utah is home to the Great Salt Lake), the New Orleans Jazz (the city is the birthplace of jazz), and the Los Angeles Hornets (so the team could keep its iconic yellow uniforms). The plan was scrapped when owners realized it might be too confusing to fans.

• The Milwaukee expansion team was still unnamed less than four months before its first games were to be played in the fall of 1970. But then the team got the first pick in the player draft, and they selected Lew Alcindor, the UCLA superstar (who would later convert to Islam and adopt the name Kareem Abdul-Jabbar). The franchise was so excited to land Alcindor that it briefly considered calling itself the Milwaukee Lews. They then realized that the moniker would be pronounced "lose."

• The Cleveland Browns of the NFL are a beloved local sports team, dating back to the 1920s. When the city got an NBA team in 1971, team owners, one of whom was local department store magnate James Henry Black, wanted to pay tribute to the Browns and actually considered calling the team the Blacks. For obvious reasons, they backed away from that choice and went with Cavaliers.

• The NBA awarded Toronto its first Canadian franchise in the fall of 1993. It was around the same time that the city had opened the 100,000-square-foot Toronto Metro Aquarium, with its prime attraction a rare white bottlenose dolphin named Toto. For the NBA team, the *Toronto Star* held a "name the team" contest, and Toronto Totos won, having received more than 45,000 nominations. But in February 1994, just three months after the aquarium opened, Toto died of a nerve disease. The Totos immediately changed names to the second-most popular entry in the contest: the Raptors (inspired by the dinosaur in the movie *Jurassic Park*).

OVERLOOKED MUSIC DELIVERY FORMATS

VInyl CDs

As compact discs became the dominant format for listening to popular music, die-hard music fans complained that the clean, crisp, digital format left them cold—it lacked the warmth, intimacy, and deep sound of a vinyl record. Engineers at Warner Bros. Records responded in 1992 by releasing a line of "Vinyl CDs." They were compact discs, playable on any standard CD player, but painted black and etched with thin grooves to resemble a record. Sonically, the recordings were digitally mastered high-quality, CD-worthy versions, but with the hissing, pops, and crackles of old records dubbed in over the music.

Earbuds

Today, iPods and all other devices come with earbud-style headphones. But the name "earbuds" was once a registered trademark—earbuds were invented by entrepreneur David "Bud" Stevenson, and they were more than just tiny, fit-in-your-ear music delivery devices. Stevenson's original EarBuds (named after himself), released in 2000, were complete, microscopic stereos. Stevenson contracted with record companies to allow EarBuds buyers to download music, for a fee, off the Internet; the music would then be wirelessly transported to and stored in the EarBuds. Apple Computer, which was developing its iPod and the launch of its digital iTunes Music Store around the same time, bought out Stevenson for a reported $300 million.

MusicLine

In the early days of home telephones, big cities offered a service whereby opera and classical music fans could pick up the phone and listen to a live performance of the local opera or symphony. One other music-by-phone system was not as popular. MusicLine was launched by a group of record labels in 1973 and was, technically speaking, one of the first "portable" music delivery systems. For a subscription fee of $6.99 a month, about the cost of a record, music fans called 1-800-MUSICLI, navigated a series of menus, and could listen to whatever they wanted to, whenever they wanted to, with no long-distance or additional phone fees. The system failed because the sound quality was poor, and less than 5 percent of Americans had the necessary touch-tone phone. Besides, the music had to be listened to alone, on a telephone receiver.

Pre-loaded Walkman

Have you ever taken a self-guided tour of a museum or historical site with a pre-loaded cassette player that walked you through the activity? That was the inspiration for music mogul David Geffen when he partnered with Sony to sell pre-loaded Walkmans in 1988. Each Walkman was decorated with pictures of a popular artist (like George Michael or Def Leppard), and the tape inside the welded-shut player would be one particular album (like *Faith* or *Hysteria*, respectively). The idea bombed due to cost: Each one-album-only Walkman cost $60. A regular Walkman was only $5 more at the time.

LITTLE-KNOWN PHOBIAS

Jonahphobia: fear of being eaten by a whale

Camouflobia: fear of being invisible

Flipperphobia: fear of dolphins

Flapperphobia: fear of fashion fads

Ondekaphobia: fear of being up to bat in baseball

Frugalphobia: fear of coupons

Onomatophoboeia: fear of things that make noises

Bleshewphobia: fear of sneezing

Pillofortaphobia: fear of unattended children

Biochemiphobia: fear of textbooks

Fibraphobia: fear of breakfast cereal

Fibberphobia: fear of being told a "little white lie"

Phsthisiophobia: fear of mispronouncing words

Stegosaurophobia: fear of the prehistoric

Ambulaphobia: fear of sirens

Sousaphobia: fear of parades

Paradoxaphobia: fear of having no fears

FORGOTTEN FAD: SOLO DATES

One of the bestselling books of 1979 was Meredith Green-field's *Love Yourself First,* a self-help book for women unlucky in love. Instead of telling women how to fix themselves or find the right man, it proposed another approach: Don't date anyone, at all, for an entire year. Instead, Greenfield argued, women should date themselves, romancing themselves and treating themselves the way they want to be treated, such as going to nice dinners, buying themselves thoughtful gifts. The object was that when they were ready to join the dating pool again, they would feel self-worth and know exactly what they wanted out of a relationship. This new, positive spin on love, dating, and self esteem was a brief cultural phenomenon, as more than 800,000 women around the world bought the book and entertained the notion of self-dating. (Greenfield parlayed her success into hosting a syndicated TV talk show called *Love Yourself First* during the 1980-81 TV season.)

Movie theaters, restaurants, and parks in the summer of 1979 were dotted with solo women (and some men) having a great time, all alone. You might have seen a person sitting at a table for two at a restaurant, talking to themselves, and laughing uproariously, or someone alone in a park cooing over a bouquet of flowers. Donna Summer's 1979 hit "Dancing On My Own" was inspired by the craze. The fad died down by 1981, when people started dating each other again.

EXTINCT DOG BREEDS

Oxocoatl Retriever

Archaeologists discovered depictions of the "Oxo" in Meso-american stone carvings. Based on the glyphs, the scientists surmised that the Oxo was a rare tree-climbing canine. It is believed that these small dogs were trained to reach the out-ermost branches of cacao plants in order to retrieve the beans that humans couldn't reach (and which monkeys often stole). Like everything else in the ancient Mayan culture, the Oxos were wiped out when the Spanish arrived.

Lithuanian Hairless

In the 14th century, while the rest of Europe was still finding its way out of the Dark Ages, Lithuania was enjoying a renais-sance of religious and scientific freedom. It was in that climate that Baltic dog breeders set out to create a new kind of animal that would share the best traits of cats and dogs. After several attempts to actually breed cats with dogs failed (the result-ing "puttens" lived for only a few hours), breeders selected canines with the most catlike qualities—a Hairless Chinese Crested and a Basenji, a mouse-hunting dog from Africa. The resulting Lithuanian Hairless was still much more doglike than catlike, but their owners treated them as if they were cats. When war later ravaged northern Europe, the selective breed-ing stopped and the breed quickly disappeared.

Regal Long-Tongue Spaniel

This breed was the result of a century of selective inbreeding by the Habsburg line of Spanish royalty. By mating the two opposite-gender puppies in each litter with the longest tongues, each successive generation got less intelligent as their tongues grew longer and longer. A portrait hanging in the Louvre depicts King Charles II of Spain (who himself had an elongated chin due to inbreeding) standing beside his Regal Long-Tongue, Dogue d'Anjou—whose tongue was nearly nine inches long. The dog's inability to eat eventually led to the extinction of the breed.

CARTOON TOWN INSPIRATIONS

Arlen, Texas – *King of the Hill*

Creator Mike Judge has said that Arlen was loosely based on conservative suburban Texas enclaves like Humble and Richardson. The name of the town where Hank Hill and his family live, however, wasn't taken from an actual place. In 1980, while attending St. Pius X High School in Albuquerque, New Mexico, Judge played trombone in a youth orchestra. There, he fell head over heels for a young harpist named Eleanor Joanna Nixon. According to friends and family, he never quite got over her and has worked references to his adolescent crush into several different projects. The character of Daria in *Beavis and Butt-Head* was based on her, and Jennifer Aniston's part in Judge's film *Office Space* was named for her. "Arlen" is an acronym that stands for "Always Really in Love with Eleanor Nixon."

Springfield – *The Simpsons*

Simpsons creator Matt Groening has never said which state the Simpsons actually live in, but has said he was inspired by the name Springfield, the non-state-specific setting of *Father Knows Best*. It's just a coincidence that Groening grew up in Oregon, which has a sizable city named Springfield. The source of its inspiration is much more literal. Jason Alexander, who played George on *Seinfeld*, explained everything in a 2009 interview with *GQ*. Like Groening, Alexander attended The Evergreen State College, a non-traditional liberal arts college in Olympia, Washington. "I ran into Matt at an alumni gathering a few years back," Alexander said. "I confronted him about the whole 'Where's Springfield?' thing and he leveled with me. As any Evergreen grad will tell you, it's named for the field next to the old Sleater iron factory." The spot in question can be found about a half mile from the campus. Evergreen students, who have used it as a setting for countless film and photo projects, call it "Spring Field" due to all of the strange, spring-related things that have been abandoned there over the years. In addition to large industrial springs from the nearby factory, which closed in 1989, it's become a dumping ground for mattresses, old car seats, and toys.

Quahog, Rhode Island – *Family Guy*

Family Guy creator Seth MacFarlane has claimed to have based Quahog (pronounced "Co-hog") on Cranston, a small town near his alma mater, the Rhode Island School of Design. While Quahog and Cranston share many locations and landmarks, the name itself is phonetic. At RISD, MacFarlane had a roommate named Patrick Henry, who owned a pot-bellied pig. In an interview with *Maxim* in 2003, MacFarlane revealed that the porker served as his muse. "Patrick's pig, Carter, was a total insomniac and stayed up with me while I worked. One time, he tried to eat my box of vintage *Playboys*. Anyway, he was my co-pilot or, in this case, my 'co-hog' so, yeah. I gave him an executive producer's credit on my thesis film project."

PROVERBS FROM AROUND THE WORLD

One finger can't hold my oxcart.

Austria

That's a fish which is hard to steer.

Japan

You need three things to live: soup, thread, and your goat.

Morocco

He that stirs the fire licks the poison.

Egypt

If you get burnt once, you're worth a horse.

Mongolia

A crying friend may simply have indigestion.

Italian

Never spend tomorrow's money in Rio.

Brazil

The trailing dog goes just as fast.

Inuit

A single eye does not travel far.

Ancient Rome

A hungry child is more than just a nail in the wall.

Nigeria

A dog will know his master's heap of cow dung.

Germany

A smiling horse eats while the caravan passes.

Tunisia

Those who wish to sing don't ask to pay the toll.

Denmark

Put silk on the goat and take it to the mayor.

France

When the sky falls, owe money.

South Africa

EARLY INCARNATIONS OF POPULAR FOODS AND DRINKS

Pink Lemonade

The Barth Brothers Circus Extraordinaire made a stop in Stockton, California, in 1935. One of the concessionaires set out a large wooden barrel full of lemonade to let the lemon juice and sugar combine. Unfortunately, a large tub of lemonade (light on the lemons, to save money) looks a lot like a big tub of water, and one of the circus's clowns tossed his red shirts in, thinking it was for staff laundry. By the time the concessionaire discovered that his lemonade had been tainted by dirty clown shirts, the circus was open and hot patrons wanted lemonade. The red shirts had colored the lemonade pink, but the vendor sold it anyway.

Salisbury Steak

During World War I, the state livery for England was located in the city of Salisbury, as it was in the eastern part of the country and a good stopping point for troops to get fresh horses before heading into the frontlines in France. The industrial cafeteria that prepared food for soldiers was also stationed in Salisbury, and due to food shortages, it didn't always have the choicest ingredients at its disposal. The livery frequently sold old or diseased horses to the food service concern, which slaughtered them, ground up the meat, and cooked it in a thick brown gravy to create a cheap meat dish called Salisbury Steak.

Dum Dums

Now a low-cost, miniature candy, Dum Dums are available in a wide variety of flavors. When they were invented by psychiatrist Dr. James Gibson in 1924, however, there was only one kind: cherry-lithium. Gibson worked at the Wormwood Sanatorium in Buffalo, New York, and oversaw the facility's most troubled residents. Gibson couldn't get these patients to take their medicines without spitting them out or throwing them out a window. So he hired his brother Hiram, a candy-maker, to create small cherry lollipops laced with a high dose of lithium, the drug used to control a variety of mental illnesses at the time. It worked. The Gibsons sold the idea, which they crudely called "Dum Dums," to a candy company in 1927, which manufactured them without the powerful psychoactive drugs for the general marketplace.

Twinkies

Contrary to urban legend, Twinkies don't last forever. For the record, they stay fresh for about 30 days. The ability to last a long time is precisely what U.S. military food scientists were after when they developed the first Twinkie in 1943. They aimed to make a compact, all-in-one meal that could last in soldiers' ration packs for weeks on end. The first Twinkie (named after chief Army food scientist Arthur Twinkleman) consisted of cooked wheat germ stuffed with deviled ham. They proved unpopular with troops, and the army sold the technology to Hostess in 1946. The baking company switched out sponge cake and cream filling for the wheat germ and deviled ham, respectively.

OFFICIAL UNICORN NAMES APPROVED BY THE INTERNATIONAL UNICORN DEPARTMENT

Contrary to popular belief, unicorns are real (see page 36), but in order to keep their magical properties in check, they are highly regulated by a worldwide governing board called the International Unicorn Department. Among the organization's duties is to ensure that every unicorn has a proper, fanciful name befitting a unicorn. This means that unicorn breeders, unicorn farm owners, and private families with a pet unicorn must use one of the entries on this strict, IUD list of approved names.

Persianna	Peach Ambrosia
Marillion	Prosecco
Minerva	Julian
Miranda	Wonderwall
Mandolin	The White Flame
Oona	Carousel Harmony
Sashay	Merrilly
Enchanté	Magic Golden Corn
Garden Feather	Sister Golden Hair
Keith	Summer Breeze
Windsong	Island Girl

Diamond Girl

Gulliver

Nightmorning

Bainbridge Island

Velveteen Esquire

Paradisio

Calamine Breeze

Lucien

Cloudpony

Forestdream

Miracle

Caspian Heartsong

Chelsea Midnight

Turbulent Indigo

Westphalia

Winterfell

Aurora Carrington

Flowersoul

Shimmer

Windracer

Dulcinea

Coriolanus

White Diamondique

Treble Clef

Rainbowlady Mountainbeam

Featherleaf

Pretty Betty

Pianissimo

Martha

Flossycurls

Cotton Candy

Dusty Wintermoon

Huckabee Velvet

Sunshower

Candyrain

Hansel

Pure Francine

Faerie-Twinkle

Eureka

Shimmer Wisp

ABANDONED APPLE COMPUTER PROTOTYPES

Muncher (1975)

The 1976 Apple I personal computer was not the first product launched by Apple. Actually, the company was launched as part of the nascent video game industry. In the early 1970s, founders Steve Jobs and Steve Wozniak sought to produce an arcade game that would "blow Pong out of the water." At the time, their concept was revolutionary and much more sophisticated than other games of the era. Muncher allowed players to control a creature that navigates a maze while eating apples and avoiding a team of malevolent worms. Unfortunately, meetings with investors didn't go as planned, so Jobs and Wozniak turned their attention toward developing computer motherboards. The prototype arcade console of Muncher disappeared before being rediscovered in, of all places, a Tokyo junk shop by a video game developer named Toru Iwatani, in 1979. He used it as an inspiration for a similar maze/chase game he was working on called Pakkuman, better known in the Western world as Pac-Man. Jobs was shocked when he encountered the game at an arcade in San Jose in 1980 but was too busy working on his company's IPO to pursue litigation.

Juicer (1984)

In 1985 Jobs found himself in a bitter power struggle with Apple's then-CEO John Sculley. Profits were down, and Jobs was saddled with much of the blame. He was ousted from his role at the company he created and resigned shortly thereafter. What's not often discussed is the chief element of their dispute. After seeing a late-night infomercial for a high-speed food dehydrator, Jobs had decided that Apple's future lay not in computers but in cutting-edge kitchen products. He and a design team created the Apple Juicer, a machine capable of turning fresh fruit into cider, juice, sauce, and even apple-flavored cereal. Jobs spent $15 million of Apple's development funds on it before he left the company.

Core (2000)

For all of its innovations in the past decade, from home computing and handheld computers, to media distribution, the area of the tech sector in which Apple has been curiously absent is home video games. Jobs rejoined the company in 2000 and enjoyed huge success with the iMac, and he began a secret game console project called Core after learning that competitor Microsoft was developing the Xbox. Instead of conventional controllers, players would have used "wands" that required them to get off their couches and move their hands and legs to interact with the games. The design team created one title before the project was canned: Fuzzy Wuzzy: Xtreme, in which a snowboarding bunny fought a weasel-like robot thief named Gates, along with his bumbling assistant Bingy, a talking stapler. After taking a hard look at the already crowded home console market, which included Sony's PlayStation and Nintendo's GameCube, Jobs cancelled the project and sold the wand concept to Nintendo, which would make it the chief feature of its Wii system.

LITTLE-KNOWN SPACE MISSIONS

Sunshots

Shortly after several *Apollo* moon trips, NASA tried to go to the sun in the 1970s. The Orpheus program (named for the Greek god Apollo's son) was not as successful as its predecessor. Orpheus 1 through Orpheus 15 were launched between 1974 and 1980, and aimed right for the sun. They were never heard from again, which suggests that either they instantly disintegrated when they got within a million miles of the sun, or none of missions have arrived yet.

Rico the Cat

Lots of animals have been spent into space: monkeys, chimps, and dogs, for example. In 1981 an orange tabby named Rico became the first cat in outer space. Rico was placed in a capsule and launched into the atmosphere. Shortly into the mission, however, Rico hit the "emergency" button, which he had been trained to press in case of emergency only, and came right back into the Earth's atmosphere, not five minutes after he'd been let out.

Frisbee Golf

The lasting image of *Apollo 14* is of astronaut Alan Shepard golfing on the moon, making a once-cool space program feel seemingly mundane. In 1975 NASA sought to recapture interest in the moon with a mission to send two astronauts to the moon to play not golf, but the exciting new sport of Frisbee golf. It would be made especially easy by the lack of the atmosphere. *Apollo 19* touched down safely on the moon in 1975, but, unfortunately, no photos of Frisbee golf on the moon exist. While the astronauts waited for their camera to warm up, they tossed the Frisbee around a bit. Edgar Mitchell threw it, but Alan Shepard didn't catch it. It sailed over his head and into outer space forever.

PRESIDENTIAL TRIVIA

• Presidents have always been, as a rule, very physically fit. Everybody knows that William Howard Taft was the least fit president, weighing more than 300 pounds. Surprisingly, the second heaviest president is Barack Obama—he weighs 285 pounds, but he's also nearly seven feet tall.

• You've seen that famous photo of Harry Truman holding up a newspaper that reads "Dewey Defeats Truman," printed after early returns showed Thomas Dewey winning the 1948 presidential election, and before Truman pulled it out in the end. Ironically, Dewey kept in all of his campaign offices, as an inspiration, a newspaper mockup that read "Truman Defeats Dewey."

• William Henry Harrison traveled everywhere in a canoe. It tended to fall over a lot, which is how Harrison earned the nickname "Tipped-a-Canoe," which was used in his 1840 presidential campaign (with John Tyler) slogan, "Tipped-a-Canoe and Tyler, too!"

• One of Ronald Reagan's last movies before he entered politics was the 1963 sci-fi B-movie *Red House*, in which aliens attack the White House and the president single-handedly fights them off and saves the world. Reagan played the president; it's what started him on his idea to become a politician.

• Calvin Coolidge was the victim of the most bizarre piece of presidential gossip ever: that he was a vampire. Why did it spread? He was extremely pale, liked to wear a cape to public appearances, eschewed eating in public, and traveled to Transylvania three times during his presidency to help broker an ultimately failed independence treaty with Romania.

• Not only was Gerald Ford the only president not elected to the job as part of a presidential ticket—he was appointed vice president by Richard Nixon when Spiro Agnew resigned, then became president when Nixon resigned—he was also the only president never to have been elected to any political office. Prior to being vice president, he'd been the Secretary of Health and Human Services, and before that he was the CEO of several insurance companies.

• Many 19th-century presidents had beards, but only one had a mustache with no beard: Grover Cleveland. Another presidential hair fact: Before Hitler made short, trim mustaches forever unfavorable, Herbert Hoover was the most famous man to wear one.

• Deeply disliked after he was voted out in 1980, Jimmy Carter laid low before deciding his next move, which was founding Habitat for Humanity in 1982. But for about 18 months between his presidency and HFH, he and his wife, Rosalynn, followed the Grateful Dead on tour, attending about 250 concerts.

WACKY LAWS

• Anyone can legally own land in New York state, but only if they hold at least a bachelor's degree.

• A horse may not run for office in Macon, Georgia, but it can be appointed to government positions.

• A Knoxville, Tennessee, law states that women out past noon must wear a yellow hat.

• It's a felony to carry live flowers in Allentown, Pennsylvania.

• Coffee may be sold no hotter than "lukewarm" in Tacoma, Washington.

• Cats must be leashed in Salem, Oregon.

• All property taxes, fines, and levies in Lansing, Michigan, must be paid entirely in coins.

• In order to buy a pet iguana in Coral Gables, Florida, law requires a five-day waiting period, four character references, and a 2,000-word written "promise of responsibility."

- In Winesburg, Ohio, robots have the right to vote.

- It's illegal to purchase alcohol between 1:00 a.m. and 1:15 a.m. in Lincoln, Nebraska.

- Felons may not buy guns in Colorado, but they are permitted to buy unlimited quantities of bullets.

- It's illegal for minors to buy cigarettes in Little Rock, Arkansas, unless they can show proof of a 4.0 grade point average.

- Tea for sale in Boston must be labeled as "English water."

- In Cedar Rapids, Iowa, any man dressed in full military regalia must legally be given a musket upon request.

- Ducks may be arrested for quacking after midnight in Topeka, Kansas.

- It's illegal to paint your home green in Greensboro, North Carolina.

- On the first day of every month, residents of Seattle are required to wear a lapel pin bearing the image of the Space Needle.

UNSOLD TV PILOTS

The Lad and the Lounge Lizard (1968)

With three seasons of his variety show, *The Dean Martin Show*, under his belt, Dean Martin decided to try a sitcom. CBS matched him up with writer-producer Sherwood Schwartz (*Gilligan's Island*), who created *The Lad and the Lounge Lizard*. It sounded like a sure thing: Martin starred as Dean Lewis, a middle-aged Las Vegas crooner who suddenly has to juggle his playboy lifestyle with parenthood when he finds out he's the father of a precocious eight-year-old (Christopher Knight, later Peter on *The Brady Bunch*), the product of a one-night stand. Martin convinced his Rat Pack cohorts Frank Sinatra and Sammy Davis Jr. to make cameos in the pilot…which is what sank the production. The trio had a fully stocked bar on the set and got drunker and drunker as the shoot went on, improvising lines, bursting into song, and making passes at female production assistants. The studio audience loved it, but the footage couldn't be aired, even in the '60s.

Grandpa Dick (1979)

After Richard Nixon resigned the American presidency in 1974, his only real source of revenue was the talk show circuit, particularly his series of interviews with British talk-show host David Frost, from which he netted $600,000. Feeling that his future lay somewhere in television, Nixon called his friend and colleague, California governor and former actor Ronald Reagan, for advice. Reagan told Nixon to give TV producer Norman Lear a call, as he had something that might be right up Nixon's alley. "I wanted another challenge along the lines of *All in the Family*," Lear told *TV Guide* in 1993. "Something even more controversial." Lear and his writers created *Grandpa Dick*, a vehicle for Nixon about the home life of a used-car salesman named Richard "Dick" Walden, living with his second wife (Mary Tyler Moore) and her liberal family in San Francsico. Nixon tackled his role with relish and loved the pilot's script, which let him make fun of hippies and Gerald Ford. However, test audiences roundly rejected the idea of Nixon in a family sitcom, and NBC didn't pick up the show. Nixon was reportedly heartbroken after hearing the news and threw himself into diplomacy work to distract himself.

Firehouse (1990)

Executives at ABC were so convinced that *Cop Rock*, their 1990 series that mixed hard-hitting police drama with Broadway-style musical numbers, would be a hit that they commissioned creator Steven Bochco to create a similar show right away. Bochco came up with *Firehouse*, which mixed the high-stakes drama of a Chicago fire team with dance numbers set to electronic "house," music. (Get it?) The pilot starred a pre-fame Brad Pitt as Donny James "D.J." Blaze, a rookie fireman constantly at odds with his older co-workers, especially Captain Jack Masters (Judd Hirsch). In a musical number that takes place inside a burning industrial plant, Pitt dances to C+C Music Factory's "Gonna Make You Sweat." In another scene, set to a song by Information Society, Masters tears up his apartment after his wife leaves him. *Firehouse* was penciled in as a midseason replacement in the 1990–91 season, but the failure of *Cop Rock* prevented *Firehouse* from sparking interest with network executives.

NOTABLE WOMEN OF THE CIVIL WAR

• Near the end of the war in late 1864, 18-year-old Confeder-ate lieutenant Aloysius Beauregard Ambrose IV was captured, along with four infantrymen, by a group of Union soldiers outside Savannah, Georgia. It was only after Ambrose had been captured that a search discovered that "he" was actually a woman who had disguised herself as a man in order to fight. Aloisa Ambrose, an only child, had left her family's farm in Cul-pepper County, Virginia, and enlisted in the Army of Northern Virginia, taking her father's name after he had been killed in the Battle of Bull Run. The morning after her capture, Ambrose died of a fever related to an infected toenail.

• High Point, Virginia, was a key resupply point for Union soldiers. The small town was protected from the Confed-eracy for nearly 18 months in part by the help of a woman named Elizabeth Joss Stanley, who sent her sons, too young to actually fight at the ages of four, five, and six, to the fields surrounding the only bridge into town. When the Stanley boys spotted Southern scouts, they would run to tell their mother, who would then coordinate the townsmen (and, as time went on, townswomen as well) to take out the scouting party and protect High Point. The town was eventually taken, shortly after the death of Mrs. Stanley, who died following a five-day bout of dysentery.

• Robert E. Lee may have fathered seven children with his wife, but he also enjoyed a long love affair with a childhood sweetheart. In letters that were not discovered until 1905, Lee wrote weekly from the front lines to Lucianna Angeline Maryford Brandeis, a portly chambermaid employed in Baltimore, Maryland. His letters often described in grim detail the brutalities of the war, all while longingly recalling the beauty of Lucianna's earlobes, neck, and crooked front tooth. Lucianna, barely literate, returned error-laden letters of her own, until two weeks before the confederate surrender and Lee's farewell letter to his troops. The last letter Lee received from Baltimore was penned by Lucianna's sister, who wrote that she "hath sadly dyed from blood loss the resolt of a byte of a badger whilst gathering well water."

• One of the nearly two thousand nurses who aided injured Civil War soldiers, Clara Josephine Wharton, 17, volunteered in the Armory Square Hospital in Washington, D.C. Clara was a friend of the poet Walt Whitman, also a volunteer nurse, who wrote in his journal about the "girl with the dove eyes and healing graces" who would sit long hours holding a wounded soldier's hand. Whitman's final journal entry mentioning Clara indicates that he was unable to attend her funeral, held on April 4, 1863. According to Whitman, she had died of a "runny nose." No other record of her death has been found.

ILL-CONCEIVED CEREAL CHARACTERS

Brainless Head. Japanese company Shiawase Shokuji produces breakfast foods and condiments as well as anatomically correct dolls called "Super Dollfie." One of those is Orokana Atama, which translates to "brainless head." With large eyes, gray skin, and flower-shaped sores on its face, the playful zombie was featured on boxes of Hai Kudaku! ("Yes Crunch!"), a red bean paste–flavored cereal sold in Japan in 2002. On the box, Orokana Atama chases children through an urban landscape, dragging his large, gangrenous foot behind.

Killer Rabbit of Caerbannog. When *Monty Python and the Holy Grail* was adapted into the Broadway musical *Spamalot* in 2005, producers sought out commercial tie-ins. They approached General Mills, producers of Count Chocula and Franken Berry, with a new monster—the film and musical's "Killer Rabbit of Caerbannog," a humorously normal-sized, but violent and bloodthirsty bunny. General Mills released a *Spamalot* cereal, which consisted of white bunny-shaped cereal bits and marshmallows with "blood" (cherry) stained mouths.

El Jefe. A nickname for Cuban dictator Fidel Castro, *El Jefe* means "the chief" in Spanish. And while cereal-maker Ralston denied it, the mascot for their 1962 cereal CubanOs was almost certainly based on him. As depicted on cereal boxes, El Jefe smiled broadly, smoked a cigar, had a long beard, and wore military fatigues. The cereal quietly disappeared from store shelves in late 1962, right after the Cuban Missile Crisis.

OBSCURE WORDS

Adoxagraphy: skilled writing on an unimportant subject

Anuria: a newborn unicorn

Bejigged: the condition of having a third nostril

Boolie: a semi-venomous Icelandic badger

Cleptobiosis: the unconscious rubbing of one's belly

Emulgent: having a runny nose

Entelectic: visibly pregnant

Farctate: to sneeze uncontrollably

Fleep: a measure of time in musical notation

Fluctuctress: the flightless pet raven of a warlock

Fusdoferiginous: wedge-shaped

Frampas: a large bag used to hold smaller bags

Gementarch: the day after tomorrow

Grampinate: to shrink in height due to old age

Griggles: the garment-industry term for buttonholes

Impignorate: to incorrectly attempt to speak with an accent

Inaniloquent: saying nothing in an artsy manner

Ingler: an adult who is consciously immature

Jument: a person's first love

Leefangs: the stitches used to close the eyes of a shrunken head

Levoduction: the birthing sounds of a mother whale

Mammothrept: one who overuses slang

Obdormition: a medieval tapestry made of human hair

Orobathymia: the desire to stare at the ocean

Oundine: pertaining to car insurance

Ouenouaoum: a word that has only one vowel

Oxter: a person who never smiles

Paludicolous: of, like, or pertaining to ducks

Predejeunist: a person who is extremely productive in the early morning hours.

Quindilliard: a government document about mineral issues

Quocunqinize: to divide into 17 equal parts

Rimestock: the industry term for the pull tab on an aluminum can

Runcation: the incorrect use of the word irony

Scrogglings: visible brushstrokes on a painting

Steatopygic: having difficulty finding a place to sit down

Tachydidaxy: the condition of having extra paws

Ugglesomnia: the urge to tuck ones pants into one's socks

Widdifulous: of, like, or pertaining to hedgehogs

FORMER COUNTRIES

Hoboland

After the transcontinental railroad was completed, and especially during the Great Depression, hobos—who led a transient lifestyle hopping trains and moving from place to place, camping out at night—were a cultural phenomenon. But hobos didn't just disappear after the Depression lifted. Instead, in the 1940s, the vast majority of North America's hobos stopped hitching rides on trains and instead stowed away on boats and made their way to Southeast Catalina Island, one of the Catalina Islands off the coast of Southern California. A hobo named Joseph "Joey Soupcan" Reynolds had learned that the island's previous landholders had skipped out on their lease and left, leaving the island uninhabited. Reynolds sent the word out to hobos around the nation to squat on Southeast Catalina Island. After 10 years, Joey Soupcan explained, squatters' rights would kick in, and the island would legally belong to the hobos. And it did. Until 1980 Hoboland was autonomous and self-governing. The society crumbled and the third-generation hobos dispersed when Baker's Beans, the third-largest canned bean company in the United States, bought the island from the hobos and turned it into a bean processing facility, which is ironic, as hobos are known for their love of beans.

745 Tiny Principalities That Now Make Up Luxembourg

The U.S. has states, Canada has provinces, and the tiny Western European nation of Luxembourg has more than 700 *quartiers*, the French word for "districts." They function like states, but unlike the states in the U.S., every single one of the

745 quartiers used to be an independent country. Modern-day Luxembourg (*luxem* means "a great many" and *bourg* means "land") was formed in 1890, following a 20-year period of unrelenting diplomacy and persuasion by Jean-Jacques Fontaine, who was the lord and reigning head of Grevenmacher, one of the most economically prominent of the micronations which were isolated from the rest of Europe by difficult-to-traverse mountain ranges. Fontaine sought greater influence in European affairs for the people of the Luxembourg region, of which 90 percent belonged to one of six prominent families and all spoke French and/or German, regardless of which of the 745 countries they were from. And while today Vatican City is technically the smallest country in the world at just 110 acres, if it were in pre-1890 Luxembourg, it would have been the third-largest country in the region. The smallest nation, Drolepetit, was roughly the size of Fenway Park.

The Moon

By the time the Soviet Union launched Yuri Gagarin into orbit in a small space module in April 1961, NASA had been formed, but the agency wouldn't be able to put a man on the moon for years. So, in order to "keep the moon warm for America's children," as NASA chief James E. Webb said in his May 1962 petition to Congress, NASA successfully convinced the United States to annex the moon. Then, in order to keep the Russians from landing on it first, President Kennedy granted the moon its independence, making the moon a country of Earth…until the United Nations ruled in 1964 that since it was all orchestrated by the U.S. as a political move, and since the U.S. was still running the "Moon government," the moon's status as a sovereign nation was invalid.

OTHER ALBUMS THAT SYNC WITH MOVIES

If you play the film *The Wizard of Oz* while listening to Pink Floyd's 1973 album T*he Dark Side of the Moon*, the two entities "sync up" repeatedly, suggesting that the band wrote the album to fit the movie. They've denied they did it on purpose, but the fact is that writing albums to classic movies was an inside joke and amusing challenge among British rock bands of that era.

The Who's *Who's Next* syncs up with *Singin' In the Rain*

A major line in "Baba O'Reilly" talks about a "teenage wasteland." This is in reference to the young movie industry depicted in the movie—it is new, but the old ways are dying with the arrival of sound in movies, signified in the song with the accordion solo. "Getting in Tune" is about the female silent-film star (Jean Hagen) who has a strange speaking voice and horrible singing voice. The big finale, where it's revealed that Debbie Reynolds's character is providing Hagen's singing voice, is what the album-ending "Won't Get Fooled Again" is about.

Led Zeppelin's *Led Zeppelin III* syncs up with *Valhalla the Valkyrie and the Mystical Quest*

Eleven different *Valhalla the Valkyrie* movies—low-budget, B-movies about a Viking warrior—were made between 1956 and 1967, and shown in England at cheap, B-movie theaters and at drive-ins in the United States. Robert Plant and Jimmy

Page loved the movies (they actually met at a 1966 screening of *Valhalla the Valkyrie vs. the Martians*), so for Led Zeppelin's third album they wrote songs based on *Valhalla the Valkyrie and the Mystical Quest*. The plot: Valhalla arrives on the icy tundra via longboat ("Immigrant Song"), runs into his best and oldest warrior friends in a tavern ("Friends"), where he flirts with a barmaid named Harper ("Since I've Been Loving You"), who is betrothed to a fearsome local warlord named Bron-Y-Aur, who challenges Valhalla to a duel on a battlefield made of ice ("Out on the Tiles"). Valhalla loses in a bloody showdown and is sentenced to death ("Gallows Pole"), but the barmaid throws a tangerine at the ropes restraining him ("Tangerine") and sets him free. Valhalla and his friends kill the warlord ("Bron-Y-Aur Stomp"), and he gets the girl ("Hats Off to Harper")

The Rolling Stones' *Exile On Main St.* syncs up with two different movies

Exile on Main St. is a double album, and each half correlates with a different movie. The first half correlates to *Willy Wonka and the Chocolate Factory*. Songs include "Rip This Joint" (about Charlie ripping open a candy bar to find a Golden Ticket to visit the Wonka factory) and "Tumbling Dice" (about Charlie and Grandpa twisting through the air when sampling a Wonka concoction). The second disc of *Exile* was written to the X-rated drama *Midnight Cowboy*, with songs about the dark, rough life of a New York street hustler, including "I Just Want to See His Face" and "Soul Survivor."

BIZARRE MILITARY PROJECTS

Bulletproof President (1793) Benjamin Franklin feared for the safety of President George Washington in the early days of the republic and so designed this "Impervious Musketball Suit." The commander in chief secretly commissioned a group of skilled blacksmiths and artisans to construct a prototype. The suit took a full year to produce and, according to documents recently uncovered in Library of Congress archives, it was a sight to behold—there was even a powdered wig attached to the helmet. The 120-pound monstrosity was intended to be worn by Washington during public appearances but proved too heavy for the aging president. Its present whereabouts are unknown.

Unicycle Corps (1917) The idea for a unicycle corps supposedly came to Secretary of State Robert Lansing in a dream during the second week of America's involvement in World War I. He envisioned a group of highly trained "super-soldiers on the world's fastest mobiles" that would "swiftly maneuver through the streets of Europe, delivering stunningly accurate vengeance." Among other things, he didn't take into account the logistics of trench warfare, in addition to the fact that no one in the U.S. military could ride one on a cobblestone street.

Project: Pretty Pretty Princess (1970) The subject of rumors around the Pentagon for decades, this project, and the incident that ensued, was proved real by documents released in 2011. The program's top-secret design team managed to create a workable "mind-control device" that used subsonic alpha waves to brainwash test subjects into believing that they were young female royals—princesses. During a test at a classified Washington, D.C. location, the device went haywire. Hours later, the project's scientists were ordered to immediately report to the White House, where they found National Security Advisor Henry Kissinger babbling in a high-pitched British accent about a missing hairbrush and being late for tea. The project was immediately canceled, and Kissinger was whisked to an unknown location for what he was told was "pony rides and cake," but what was really 96 hours of deprogramming.

Non-Lethal Muck Cannon (1861) This weapons project, devised by the Lincoln administration during the first weeks of the Civil War, sought to bring a quick end to the conflict while injuring as few Confederate soldiers as possible. After early trials proved promising, then-commanding general Winfield Scott organized a recycling program, the first of its kind, to make use of his battalions' bacon grease, food scraps, tobacco spit, and droppings. Combined with watery mud and placed in thin, burlap bags, these ingredients composed the cannon's "muckballs." While the shells would have likely proven capable of disabling large swaths of troops, further tests proved that conventional ballistics of the era were ill equipped to deliver the disgusting payload with precession. A last-ditch effort to salvage the project with a revised steam-powered catapult resulted in disaster. During an experiment, the weapons's delivery arm snapped, covering several military scientists in muck.

UNAIRED TV SPINOFFS

Dancing Without the Stars

Even when the "stars" on *Dancing With the Stars* aren't very well known, the show is still among the top five most-watched shows on TV. To ABC, this meant that the most popular part of the show wasn't the stars, but the dancing. In 2007 it produced a pilot for *Dancing Without the Stars*, in which its hired stable of dancers danced solo routines each week for points from the enthusiastic panel of judges.

Stars

Alternately, the stars that had been hired for a round of *Dancing With the Stars* were put in a green room and filmed, just chatting and drinking chai lattes, for a spinoff of *Dancing Without the Stars* called simply *Stars*. Due to the involvement of Frank Stallone, who is a huge celebrity in Estonia, the show aired once, in Estonia.

Deadwood Kids

In 2005, the Old West drama *Deadwood* was a smash hit on HBO. But it was too violent, too full of prostitutes, and too full of Shakespearean dialogue and profanity to ever be a crossover hit with the demographic that likes the Old West more than anyone: little boys. So HBO asked *Deadwood* creator David Milch to make a cartoon version for kids called *Deadwood Kids*. At Deadwood Day Care Center, Al Swearengen (voice of Ian McShane) no longer keeps the town plied with booze and hookers; instead, he controls the illicit juice-box trade and determines which girls will get to push which boys on the swings, all under the watchful eye of playground safety monitor Seth Bullock (voice of Timothy Olyphant).

Wheel of Fortune Nights

After helping contestants spin a large wheel and solve simple word puzzles, Pat Sajak and Vanna White don trench coats and team up to solve mysteries.

Top Chef: Pica Challenge

Pica is a medical condition, experienced primarily by pregnant women and people lacking proper nutrition in extremely poor areas of the world, that causes the craving of inedible objects like dirt, rocks, and hair. This *Top Chef* spinoff saw America's most talented and famous chefs using these items to create the most appetizing meals possible.

The Real Housewives of Deadliest Catch

On paper, it seemed like this show was a winner, combining the two most successful reality TV phenomena of recent years: bored spouses hanging out, and fishermen. It didn't work out—*The Real Housewives of Deadliest Catch* was, indeed, deadly. The actual wives of the fishermen were filmed for two weeks, but they did little beyond sitting around and quietly worrying if their husbands were alive. Once in a while, somebody looked out a window or cried silently to herself.

DEPRESSION ERA PASTIMES

During the Depression, Americans were financially and emotionally downtrodden, and they craved entertainment that could last a whole night, but cost only pennies. A lot of choices sprang up: dance marathons, and roller derby, for example. Here are some others that time has forgotten.

Feats of Counting

Numberists, a term coined by vaudeville star Marcus the Amazing Numberist, would simply count as high as they possibly could. It may sound boring, but they did it with flourish. Marcus, for example, would deliver each number in a loud, deep voice, and pause dramatically before reciting the next one. Then, he might say the next number in a quiet or silly voice. Marcus's shows would go on for three or more hours, during which he'd sometimes reach 1,000 or higher.

Being Still

Ever play that childhood game where you see who can lie still the longest? That was a thing adults did during the Depression. They would lie perfectly still for as long as possible, until they got bored or restless, or they twitched. Stillness contests were frequently held between shows at double-feature movies: Participants, who paid a nickel each to compete could take home around $5 to $10 for being the winner.

Talking-Animal Plays

Speakers were fitted on collars and placed around the necks of dogs, cats, pigs, and horses. The animals were then shoved out onto a stage, where they walked around, dressed in costume as characters from Shakespeare plays. Offstage, human voices read lines from the plays that were being "acted out" by the animals. It was a very popular from of entertainment, combining the grandeur of Shakespeare with animals wandering off and pooping a lot.

COCA-COLA'S BIGGEST MISTAKES

Coke4

Jolt Cola was briefly popular in the early 1980s—it had double the caffeine of a regular can of cola, but the same amount of sugar, and was marketed as a coffee alternative. Coca-Cola responded with Coke4 in 1984. It was Coca-Cola with four times as much caffeine and four times as much sugar, giving the drinker a far bigger jolt than Jolt. One can had 156 grams of sugar and 400 milligrams of caffeine—more sugar than six Twinkies and more caffeine than five cups of coffee. It was banned in 11 states, while the state of New York wouldn't sell it to anyone under 21. The restrictions hurt sales, and Coca-Cola stopped production of Coke4 just two years later.

Newer Coke

The 1985 launch and quick failure of New Coke is one of the biggest flops and cautionary tales in business history. A quick recap: Losing sales to Pepsi, Coca-Cola reformulated its iconic recipe to be sweeter, like Pepsi. Some people think it was all an elaborate publicity stunt, or when Coca-Cola Classic was discontinued and brought back, it was to mask the fact that sugar had been replaced in the beverage with high-fructose corn syrup. But New Coke did have some fans—in the Philippines, for example. Pepsi had dominated the soda market there, until New Coke took Coke's market share from 5 to 80 percent, destroying Pepsi. New Coke stayed on the market in the Philippines until 1991, when Coke amazingly repeated the American New Coke debacle in the Philippines, replacing New Coke with a reformulation of *that* product called Newer Coke. It bombed, and Coca-Cola restored the old New Coke in less than three weeks.

Tab−

Coca-Cola manufactures Tab, one of the first low-calorie sodas to hit the market, available since 1972. Tab has since been overshadowed by myriad other diet colas, but every few years, Coke tries to rebrand and relaunch it; there was even a clear version to compete with Crystal Pepsi in 1993. In 2003 Coke introduced Tab− ("Tab Minus"), "the first cola to help you lose weight." For while other diet drinks had zero calories, Tab− was made with ingredients like green tea extract and celery root powder—foods that take more calories for the body to burn than are in the foods themselves. In other words, they're "negative calories" that result in negligible weight loss. It failed to catch on, as people who tried it said it tasted like "carbonated V8."

Tab Xtreme

Tab had always been marketed to women—it's a "diet" drink that comes in a pink can. In 2009, however, Coca-Cola unveiled Tab Xtreme, targeted to men. It was exactly the same drink, but it came in a silver-and-black double-size can made of steel. Guys, or hardly anyone at all, bought it.

ORIGINS OF HOLIDAY TRADITIONS

Santa Claus

In Italy, the tradition of gifts being delivered to children by a stranger who comes in through the chimney takes a different face than that of the familiar and fleshy man in red. Instead, on Epiphany Eve, Befana, an old woman riding a broom, comes to deliver candy and presents to good children and fill the socks of bad children with coal. Rather than leaving out milk and cookies for Befana, families will leave out a dinner plate and a glass of wine. Some folklorists have suggested that Befana stems from the Roman goddess Strina, but a popular Italian psychologist wrote that the tradition "is a clear manifestation of anxiety related to the tradition of powerful Italian mothers and grandmothers. The old woman steals into the house, ready to reward good children, punish 'bad ones,' and even clean the house with her broom, suggesting that Italian housewives are inferior—it's a sad commentary on the Italian psyche." Nevertheless, Befana is clearly a predecessor to the Santa mythos.

Easter baskets

While common legend claims that Easter baskets have been used for centuries in pagan celebrations of spring, their origin can actually be traced to a 17th-century English basket maker named Reed. Reed lived in the Suffolk town of Ipswich and operated his business with the help of his 14 sons. Reed was a renowned businessman and unprecedented marketer who, by tying both springtime and the Christian tradition of Easter to the procurement of baskets filled with eggs and candy, turned his basket-making business into a small empire. All officially sanctioned Easter baskets are still made by Reed's descendents.

Chinese New Year dumplings

It's commonly held that the round dumplings served as part of traditional Chinese New Year festivities represent the full moon, perfection, and family unity. But in 1996, a Chinese history scholar at the Tsinghua University in Beijing discovered numerous documents that suggest another origin for the dumplings. The Chinese scholar Huangfu Mi, who lived 215–282 A.D., wrote extensively about the dumplings as a representation not of the full moon, but of a full breast, engorged with milk. (The perfection and family unity thing still works.)

The giving of ties for Father's Day

Up until the mid-20th century, fathers got their sons presents on Father's Day. If his son turned 15 that year, he was given a tool representing the father's trade (a set of roofing tools for a roofer, a spatula for a cook, etc.). It was a nice way to pass the torch, and to shepherd a son into adulthood and working life. By the 1950s, offices became the dominant place of business in the U.S., so men started giving their sons ties. Over the next thirty years later, the practice gradually reversed, and sons began giving their dads neckwear on Father's Day.

STATE NAME ORIGINS

• **Louisiana** was not named after King Louis XIV of France. French explorer Rene-Robert Cavalier named it for his cook, Louise.

• Dutch settlers meant to name their territory "New Vader" (Vader means "father"), but sloppy handwriting led it to being called "**Nevada**."

• Conventional wisdom says that Indianapolis means "Indiana-city." Not true. The state of **Indiana** was named by its first settler, a Greek farmer named Niko Indonopoulis.

• **Oregon** was once an unnamed region of California, filled with iron ore mining operations. By 1859, the mining companies folded, and most of the population moved out when the "ore was gone."

• Remember the Maine? In 1898 the American warship the U.S.S. Maine sank near Cuba, igniting the Spanish-American War. Two years later, when New Hampshire split into two states, the new area was named **Maine**, in deference to the ship, which in turn was named for the French port city of Maine, which has been building warships for three centuries.

• Initially inhabited by the Iroquois, **Minnesota** is the combination of two Iroquois words: *minesa*, which means "cold place," and *sattah*, which means "wet."

• To celebrate a new baby, French villagers traditionally gather in the town square for a 24-hour religious festival called the *misoeur*. When the first French immigrants arrived in what is now St. Louis, they held a misoeur to christen their new territory, which they named after their old tradition. The word was eventually anglicized into **Missouri**.

• **Arkansas** got its name from a group of Irish immigrants who originally headed west to settle in the Kansas Territory. They found good land before they reached their destination and called it East Kansas. In Irish it's pronounced "Hawr-Kansah."

• The Spanish founders of **Texas** came to the area to make use of the clay-rich soil around the Rio Grande. Clay is an important ingredient in the manufacturing of *tejas*, the Spanish word for "ceramic tiles."

• There have long been two Virginias, but until about 100 years ago, they were East Virginia and West Virginia. In 1897, Virginia O'Hanlon wrote a letter to the *New York Sun*, which prompted the famous "Yes, Virginia, there is a Santa Claus" response editorial. The story became a cultural phenomenon, and to attract attention and tourists, East Virginia changed its name to, simply, **Virginia.**

MORE STRANGE MEDICAL CONDITIONS

Kurkov Syndrome. The condition was discovered in 1974 when a Soviet diamond smuggler named Yuri Kurkov swallowed his loot to avoid being caught (although he was captured and detained anyway). Authorities waited for him to pass the diamonds, but he never did...nor did they show up on X-rays or body scans. The conclusion: Kurkov had the ability to digest diamonds. He admitted to swallowing diamonds to avoid capture on at least five other occasions.

Schneider-Brno Elbow Mutation. It's impossible for most humans to lick their own elbows, except for the Schneider family from Brno in the Czech Republic. Biologists at the Abbey of St. Thomas in Brno have been studying the family since 1875, when an Augustinian monk first noticed the family's quirky ability. The monk's name was Gregor Mendel, whose systematic hybridization of pea plants laid the foundation for modern genetics. Scientists don't see any evolutionary advantage for licking one's elbow, but the Schneiders, who today own a chain of pubs, regularly earn money by winning bar bets.

Pen Location Anomaly. Because of a mutation of her chromosome 10, 36-year-old Baltimore, Maryland, woman Ann Carolle can tell within two feet the location of every pen she's ever touched. "It's like a memory. I just know where it is. I can even tell you about some that I was near but didn't use."

THE SALINGER VAULT

J.D. Salinger is as well known for being reclusive as he was for writing *The Catcher in the Rye*, one of the definitive novels of the 20th century. That's about all he published…but that doesn't mean he stopped writing. Upon Salinger's death, in 2010, lawyers confirmed the existence of the following works in his vault.

Harold and the Pyramid of Fish (1985)

Scribbled notes in the margins of this screenplay reveal that, at one point, Salinger was plotting a return to Hollywood after decades of bitterness surrounding *My Foolish Heart*, the "bastardized" 1949 film adaptation of his short story "Uncle Wiggily in Connecticut." Letters to close friends indicate that he watched a lot of movies. In one note, he expressed his disgust for *Raiders of the Lost Ark* (1981), which he said "might be excused for its unwitty, unfunny, awful socko-ness if it had been put together by *Harvard Lampoon* seniors." Regardless, it was an obvious inspiration for Salinger's *Harold and the Pyramid of Fish*, a send-up of action films. "Harold is a tough guy," Salinger wrote in the script. "He wears an old bomber coat with worn leather boots and a wide-brimmed hat that he never takes off." The plot follows Harold's quest for "the fabled bananafish" (a reference to one of the entries in his collection *Nine Stories*), a mystical object capable of "gobbling up the world's entire fruit supply." Along the way, he encounters an array of Nazis, phonies, cheeseburger stands, jazz pianists, and the psychotic host of a radio quiz show."

Signatures (2008)

Many of Salinger's fans have sought his autograph over the years—given his self-imposed sequestration, it's pretty difficult to come by. According to one report, copies of his signature can fetch anywhere between $700 and $2,500 at auction, even more than Abraham Lincoln's. As documents found in a manila folder in the vault reveal, Salinger found this "incredibly comical" and wanted to produce a limited-edition series of 100 small books consisting of nothing but his signature. "I'm thinking twenty pages each with my name appearing five times on each one. By my math, that comes out to 10,000 autographs. That should flood the market, all right, and drop the price down quite a bit. I just hope this old hand of mine will be able to, well, handle this Herculean task. I'll call this one *Signatures*. Seems apt."

When a Body Meets a Body (1970s, 2009)

Literature experts long theorized that Salinger wrote a sequel to *The Catcher in the Rye*, and that he came out of seclusion in early 2009 to stop the publication of an unauthorized sequel by Swedish author Fredrik Colting. "This fight has invigorated my withering bones," Salinger wrote in a journal found in the vault. "I must dig out *Body* and finish it. I haven't even looked at those pages since the oil embargo. There's still so much for the boy to say and I tire of these walls. It's high time I get out there one last time before Death comes for me." The book catches up with Holden Caulfield in 1976, now approaching 40 and even more disgusted with the modern world than when he was a teenager. He calls in sick to his job as a gym teacher at Pencey Prep and spends the day wandering the streets of Manhattan, chatting with its denizens and brooding about everything from Wall Street bankers to punk rockers. Holden winds up at a screening of *Deep Throat* in a seedy theater in Times Square before the novel leaps forward in time to find him in a nursing home in 2009. He slips out one afternoon to take "one last spin on the carousel in Central Park, the one that Phoebe liked so much." The manuscript ends, mid-sentence, with Holden standing in line with a group of school children on a field trip. By all indications, Salinger's declining health got the better of him, leaving the ultimate fate of his most famous character as enigmatic as the author himself.

Cooking, the Salinger Way (1999)

Salinger reportedly had a proclivity for homeopathic medicine and engaged in obsessive eating habits, which led to him to pen a cookbook. This strange, 270-page manuscript offers exhaustive recipes for incredibly simple dishes. There's an entire chapter devoted to frozen peas, one of Salinger's favorite foods, which he often ate for breakfast. "The pea is, quite simply, nature's most perfect edible, especially on ice," Salinger wrote in the book's introduction. "It may as well be manna from heaven. It's a shame that more people don't down a plate of them with their morning cup of joe. I, myself, like to stick frozen peas right in my coffee pot." Other recipes in the book include tips on how to "properly under-cook lamb burgers" and why "half a fifth of cobra whiskey a day helps keep the doctor away."

VIDEO-GAME ADAPTATIONS OF MOVIES AND TV SHOWS

Hoarders

Even though it's one of the most watched and familiar shows on cable TV, it's hard to merchandise a show that's more or less about gawking at the suffering of others. And yet, in this video game the player controls the member of a clean-up crew, packing junk into trash bags. Points are awarded finding gold coins among the stacks of newspapers, yogurt tubs, and dead cats.

The Blind Side

One would assume that a video-game version of the Best Picture–nominated drama about a rich woman who adopts an African-American football phenom would be mostly about football, but there isn't any of that. One of the movie's major scenes involves the main character searching the Memphis housing projects for her adopted son, who had ran away after a fight, and the game recreates that.

The Breakfast Club

Released to arcades in 1985, the game was little more than a (barely) reworked version of unsold Ms. Pac-Man machines. Instead of a yellow ball eating white pills, players controlled a tiny, pixelated image of Molly Ringwald's face, which raced around the board while a tiny, pixelated image of Judd Nelson chased her.

Downton Abbey

From the game's box: "Play as Matthew and survive German shelling attacks in World War I, or play as the Dowager Countess and defeat enemies with withering remarks. Watch out for changing social mores (and lasers)!"

When Harry Met Sally

This game picks up on the movie's essential premise that "men and women can't be friends without falling in love," as Harry chases Sally around New York City, gobbling pastrami sandwiches for energy and throwing hearts at her. For some reason, Harry rides a pet dinosaur.

The Golden Girls vs. Designing Women

Those brassy Southern dames from Sugarbaker Interior Design take a road trip to Miami, where they break into Rose, Dorothy, Blanche, and Sophia's house and steal a cheesecake out of their freezer. It's up to the old ladies to track down the *Designing Women* women and get back that cheesecake, as it's actually the Eterna Key, a magical talisman that would end time and life as we know it if it fell into the wrong hands.

Being John Malkovich

Not really an adaptation so much as it was inspired by the 2004 art film, the game is made up of mini-games like "John Malkovich's Puppet Workshop" and "Make John Malkovich Act Weird on the Street."

GROSS BUT REAL COCKTAILS

The Jagger-Meister

The name is, of course, a play on the name of Jagermeister, the licorice-flavored German liqueur. A Jagger-Meister however, is named for British rock star Mick Jagger, and is about the most "British" cocktail imaginable: It's made from Newcastle Brown Ale, Pims, brown sauce, and blood-pudding-flavored schnapps, and garnished with "chips," the British term for French fries.

The Ham Salad

A vodka martini made with a splash of liquid from a canned ham instead of sweet vermouth, and garnished with a cube of ham on a toothpick.

High Holy Day

It's a combination of religiously oriented ingredients: one part Benedictine (a French liqueur created by Catholic monks), one part Manischewitz kosher wine, and one part green tea, long connected with Zen Buddhism.

Hulk Hogan

Orange juice and grenadine (for a yellow-and-red color combination, like Hogan's '80s-era costume) along with rum and a float of anabolic steroids.

Dirty Policeman

It gets its name because it is somewhat blue, like a police-man's uniform, and somewhat brown, like dirt. One part whiskey to three parts Berry Blue Kool-Aid, it's served over ice, with a mini-doughnut garnish. (A "Security Guard" is a similar cocktail, with milk added in to make the drink gray, like a security guard's uniform.)

Back to School

The base ingredient is milk, because kids going to school would drink milk, along with ground-up cookies, chocolate-flavored liqueur, and a ground-up crayon.

Easter Sunday

A light white wine (usually Chardonnay) with chocolate eggs dropped in, garnished with a spiral-cut hard-boiled egg.

Taco Tuesday

A taco with all the fixings combined in a blender, poured into a shot glass, and followed with a tequila chaser and a wedge of lime.

The Cheese Plate

Intended as an after-dinner drink, this cocktail combines blue cheese-flavored schnapps with aged gouda-infused vodka. It's traditionally garnished with a slice of Swiss cheese.

OBSCURE CABLE CHANNELS

Amish Life

Amish Life (1992–1994) broadcast how-to instructional shows on butter churning, barn-raising, and livestock. (It also

showed movies as filler, as most cable networks do, particularly the Harrison Ford movie *Witness*.) The network was a huge flop—very few Amish have electricity, let alone cable TV.

Boat Club

This low-rent station is available on just a handful of cable systems on the East Coast. All shows are filmed on and broadcast from a degrading yacht that's permanently docked in a harbor in Wilmington, North Carolina. Taking on a public-access feel, the channel's programs are hosted by "Captain Bill" Northcutt. He was the captain of a garbage barge that crashed into a beach on Prince Edward Island in 1998; although he had been drinking at the time, he won a large cash settlement from the barge company, which he used to fund Boat Club. Captain Bill drinks on air, swilling from a large bottle of brown liquid he calls "Boat Club Original Recipe." He offers it to his guests, who include boat builders, boat racers, boat enthusiasts, and boat collectors. Between interview segments, Boat Club shows short films about famous boats. It broadcasts five hours of original programs each day, which are then repeated four times. The remaining schedule consists of reruns of cheaply available boat-themed movies, such as *Overboard*.

The Silver Channel

Market research by communications giant Viacom showed that Americans over the age of 75 watch more TV than any other demographic. So Viacom launched the Silver Channel to appeal to older viewers. Its programming included reruns of Andy Rooney's commentary segment from *60 Minutes*; a talk show called *Remember When?* hosted by Art Linkletter, which featured the TV personality interviewing senior citizen celebrities and asking them about "the good old days"; and *Pictures of My Grandkids*, which consisted of photos of grandchildren sent in by viewers. (It also showed movies as filler, as most cable networks do, particularly *The Best Years of Our Lives*.) When it debuted in 2002, ratings for the Silver Channel placed it on par with CNN, ESPN, and HBO, the most-watched networks on cable TV. But then the network took a phone poll and realized that the vast majority of its viewers fell asleep with the TV on. The channel died quietly in 2003.

Tragedy Central

Comedy Central is the only surviving member of a trio of similarly branded networks that debuted in 1991. Gone is the MTV clone Music Central, as is Tragedy Central. While

Comedy Central succeeded as a niche for comedic shows and movies, Tragedy Central was supposed to be a place for serious, and often incredibly depressing, dramatic movies, war documentaries, and charity telethons. Every Sunday it played a marathon of Ingmar Bergman movies.

Tooth!

Tooth! focuses on dental themes and oral hygiene-oriented programming. It presents instructional shows on flossing, brushing, and toothpicks, as well as reruns of dentist-themed movies like *The Marathon Man*.

NetNet

The Henderson Net Company of Toluca Lake, New York, is a billion-dollar corporation, as it's the official supplier of nets and netting to the NBA, NHL, Major League Soccer, and several large commercial fishing concerns. As a way to generate further interest in nets, it poured a lot of its profits into a cable channel called the Net Network, or NetNet. The channel airs a lot of net-based sports, including college badminton, European tennis, high-school volleyball, New Jersey Nets home games, as well as reruns of fishing shows like *Deadliest Catch*. (It also shows movies as filler, as most cable networks do, particularly the 1995 Sandra Bullock thriller *The Net*.)

MORE RANDOM BITS OF KNOWLEDGE

• Bestselling recording artist of all time in Iraq: Pat Boone.

• *Mad* magazine mascot Alfred E. Newman is based on a photo of famed publisher William Randolph Hearst as a teenager.

• There are more Chuck E. Cheese game tokens in circulation than there is Finnish currency.

• By weight, carrots have more vitamin C than oranges.

• Restaurants used to serve just one course each. You'd go to one for soup, another for the salad, another for bread, one for the entree, and one for dessert if you wished.

• *The Price Is Right* theme song is a sped-up, lyric-less version of a Vietnam War–protest folk song.

• Actress Melissa Joan Hart was named after Melissa and Joan Rivers, her mother's favorite celebrities.

• Sugar substitute Sweet'N Low is actually napalm with just one molecule added.

BIZARRE PLAYS OF THE 1990s

Millie (1992)

An NYU graduate student who used the pen name Winchester Winechest (his real name was never disclosed) wrote and produced his first and only play, which supposedly depicted the presidency of George H.W. Bush from the point of view of Millie, the president's Springer Spaniel. The book was inspired by the 1990 publication of *Millie's Book: As Dictated to Barbara Bush*. The star of the show, a 25-year-old Juilliard-trained actor named Katherine Spencer-Pratt, spent the entirety of the 146-minute play crawling the stage on all fours. The second act of the play included an extended monologue by Millie comprising howls, grunts, whines, barks, and licks. In the final scene, Spencer-Pratt spent more than two minutes licking the feet of the actress portraying Barbara Bush.

Gigantic Weekend (1999)

Critics universally panned *Gigantic Weekend*, a rip-off of the 1978 cult-classic surfing film *Big Wednesday*. The playwright, Rick Melon, had been warned by friends that a stage play about surfing might not be as effective as a filmed-on-location movie, but he persisted. The director was likewise warned that the actor who played the off-the-wall character inspired by Gary Busey's turn in *Big Wednesday* would have a hard time delivering dialogue while wearing cartoonishly large false teeth. Those warnings went unheeded. The show ran at a church-turned-theater in Queens for only two nights.

My Broken Cervix, Vols. 1–17 (1996)

As part of the thriving feminist art movement of the 1990s, a group of women performers staged a series of 17 one-act plays featuring gynecological themes. In one, the protagonist spends the majority of the play sitting on a toilet. In another, a group of women in bodysuits beat another woman in a nightclub restroom for asking to borrow a tampon. One of the collaborators, Alice Whitehead, said in a 1998 interview in *Rain and Thunder: A radical feminist journal of discussion and activism* that she felt the playwright Eve Ensler, author of *The Vagina Monologues*, "has never owned up to the fact that there were other pioneers in the realm of vaginally-themed theater—though, honestly, we always preferred the term 'vulva.' If it weren't so sad I'd be angry."

Miss Panzarella Bakes a Pie (1991)

The main character, scorned by her lover, steals her neighbor's cat and bakes it into a pie. The audience does not get to find out what happens to the kitten pie, as the lights go down as the heroine leaves her apartment, pie in hand. The play, performed in silent pantomime, consisted of long scenes in which Miss Panzarella actually made a pie crust from scratch, including five minutes during which the actress (who also performed in the nude) rested the dough in the refrigerator and appeared to be watching a silent television. While star Penelope Furnace has since scorned the play as "ridiculous," reviewers at the time disagreed. *New York Magazine* said the production was "an absolute revelation on the topics of female sexuality vis-à-vis dough, and an indictment of the male gaze."

ORIGINS OF THE WONDERS OF THE WORLD

The Pyramids of Egypt

Ancient texts and diagrams discovered in the mid-1920s by Howard Carter, the same man who discovered the tomb of King Tut, indicated that the gigantic pyramids were actually intended to be cubes. Scholars are still trying to decipher the so-called "Blueprint Scrolls," but it's clear that the ancient Egyptians were not as advanced in math as their contemporaries in China or the Middle East. And as one archaeologist told *Time*, "It's hard to create a building that looks the way you want it to look without math."

The Great Wall of China

Contrary to popular belief, the Great Wall of China is actually a natural occurrence, dating back to movements of ice and tectonic plates in the most recent glacial period, the Pleistocene (about 150,000 years ago). Qin Shihuang, king of the state of Qin during China's Warring States period, was the first to build a watchtower on the natural formation and claim that his people had built the wall sometime around the year 230 B.C. as a way of establishing a claim to his people's dominance. Subsequent rulers took up the idea, and the myth has followed the wall into the popular imagination.

The Grand Canyon

Another popular misrepresentation of nature is Arizona's Grand Canyon. While there was originally a canyon naturally present, it was less than three miles long and reached a width of only half a mile at its widest point. The canyon was actually torn to its current length of more than 200 miles in a spectacular post-Civil War show of dynamite force as a publicity stunt, part of a celebration for the 1919 announcement of Grand Canyon National Park. A series of massive explosions went on for nearly an hour and, as a local newspaper reported, "rent the earth asunder in a terrifying temblor felt for hundreds of miles." The initial explosions and their aftershocks even diverted the Colorado River to its current location—it had run several miles northwest of its current trajectory before the explosions.

The Colosseum

The original Roman colosseum was accidentally torn down by a misinformed construction crew in 1912. All crew members were quickly jailed, and the work boss was put to death by hanging the following month. The replica Colosseum, which still stands today, was rebuilt and artificially aged in a five-year project, the largest public works project in Italian history.

The Northern Lights

In 2007, scientists were shocked to discover that the Northern Lights are not natural. The lights are part of a chain reaction that involves the mantle layer of the earth's core, but which originate with the use of electricity and ground wires. This finding correlated with historians' puzzlement over the absence of any mention of the light show in any documents prior to 1925.

FORGOTTEN FAD: MULTIPLE FACIAL MOLES

In the 18th century, the French bourgeoisie considered it the height of fashion to have a mole—it was thought that the extra mass of tissue and pigment on the face was a sign of health and abundance, that the person with a mole had so much flesh that it was literally bursting out of the face. Fake moles became fashionable as a way to imply status and wealth. But soon nearly every Parisian had a facial mole, making it impossible to tell who the true elite were anymore.

So the French royals, nobles, and super-wealthy took to wearing secondary moles. But they weren't exactly "fake"—they were cut off of the faces of servants or made of compressed horsehair. Like single moles, multiple moles became popular with the masses. To stay ahead, the upper classes added more and more moles, and by the time of the French Revolution, it was common for a member of French high society to sport at least 15 facial moles. Marie Antoinette, for example, had more than 40.

THE ORIGIN OF RAP MUSIC

In 1975, 19-year-old Reggie DeWitt was working as an intern at Atlantic Records in their Miami studio. His main tasks were to keep the recording booths clean and fetch coffee and lunch for the Bee Gees while they recorded their album *Main Course*. One day, the Gibb brothers came in with an idea for a song with a hard-charging, bass-driven disco beat, modeled after the chugging noise their car made as it crossed a Miami bridge on the way to the studio. They called it "Drive Talking," but soon altered it to "Jive Talkin'," after the name of the urban slang of the era.

As he delivered coffee, DeWitt perked up when he heard the Bee Gees talking about "jive." He'd grown up in Brooklyn, where jive was spoken as much as English. DeWitt and his friends particularly liked to speak to each other in rapidly delivered rhyming jive, trying to top each other with clever rhymes and wordplay. After the band went home after a recording session, DeWitt snuck into the studio and recording himself rhyme-jive-talking over the pounding beat of the Bee Gees' demo of "Jive Talkin'." He only made it about two minutes before producer Arif Mardin came in and told him to "wrap it up."

Knowing that the soundalike word "rap" was another word for informal speech, like jive, DeWitt called his experiment "rap." Some homemade demos became the first rap music heard in public when he gave them to house-party DJs back home in Brooklyn about two years later.

FLAG DAY CHARACTERS

Part of why Christmas, Easter, and Valentine's Day are major holidays is because they're associated with widely recognizable characters: Santa Claus, the Easter Bunny, and Cupid, respectively. If a holiday doesn't have a mascot, it's relegated to obscurity—like Flag Day.

The Flag Day Foundation (FDF) formed in 1975, just before the huge U.S. Bicentennial celebration, with the mission statement to "Elevate Flag Day, June 14th, to the major holiday status it deserves, as it celebrates the Stars and Stripes as a symbol of America and American ideals, and is just as good as the Fourth of July." In the past four decades, the FDF has tried—and failed—to generate interest in Flag Day, primarily by introducing Flag Day characters.

1975: Flaggy

The first FDF mascot was a humanlike, anthropomorphic flag with arms, legs, and big cartoonish eyes. (He was designed by artists at the Hanna-Barbera TV cartoon studios) Flaggy did poorly in focus-group testing, as children said they didn't understand how a piece of cloth could be alive, while adults thought it was disrespectful to America. *Flaggy and the Flag Day That Almost Wasn't: A Flag Day Special* aired on Flag Day Eve on CBS and became the lowest-rated holiday special in TV history (until it was beaten eight years later with the 1983 broadcast of *A Very Smurfy Purim*).

1980: Flag Day Fanny

Around this time, 1920s culture was experiencing a revival in America, so the FDF introduced Fanny, a '20s-style flapper in bobbed hair and a short, American-flag print dress. She talked in a high-pitched voice, similar to that of Betty Boop. After the flapper fad died down six months later, millions of unsold Fanny T-shirts and dolls were buried in a New Mexico landfill.

1985: Chekov the Dinosaur

With pro-American spirit at a high following the landslide reelection of Ronald Reagan, the FDF tried to put the failures of Flaggy and Flag Day Fanny behind it by introducing a new character: Chekov. He starred in a comic book called *Chekov the Dinosaur Learns the Error of His Ways*, distributed free to more than 20 million kids just before the end of the school year in early June. In the comic, Chekov, a dinosaur from Dinosauristan, an obvious substitute for a Soviet republic, comes to Flagland (a stand-in for the U.S.) and, overwhelmed by the thousands of American flags waving everywhere he goes, eats one. He's arrested and sentenced to a time-traveling trip through American history, where he learns what the flag truly means. At the end, he renounces his citizenship in Dinosauristan and becomes a flag maker in Flagland.

2008: Zombie-Killing Betsy Ross

The FDF disbanded in 1987, but reformed in 2006. Hoping to cash in on the late 2000s "zombie craze," the organization launched an Internet campaign centered around its new character, Zombie-Killing Betsy Ross. A series of animated YouTube videos depicted the designer and creator of the first American flag fighting off the undead, walking corpses of enemies of America from the 1700s up through Osama Bin Laden. Like all Internet fads, the Zombie-Killing Betsy Ross videos were loved by millions for a few months...then never spoken of again.

THREE REAL WIZARDS

Sir Isaac Newton

Newton ensured his place in history when an apple fell on his head and he came up with the Universal Law of Gravitation, which states that the force gravity between two objects depends on the masses of those objects and the distance between their centers. Scientific research began as a front for Newton's real pastime, wizardry, which he worked on only late at night. He rarely went to bed until five or six in the morning, spending hours transforming copper into gold and concocting his "Elixir of Immortality," of which the main ingredient was donkey urine. (It didn't work—Newton died in 1727.) Newton was able to keep a lot of his wizardry secret because he used a seemingly nonsensical personal shorthand to write his notes, which were really spells. "The magic fire of the king's bath, when drained of bubbles causes twice the troubles," read one passage, which reportedly allowed the impotent British king James II to father seven children. Newton also reportedly summoned a genie to swallow the Plague of 1644 and grew sterling silver flowers in his Cambridge house.

Thomas Edison

Edison was nicknamed "The Wizard of Menlo Park" after a New Jersey reporter witnessed Edison's most recent invention, the photograph. The reporter had no idea that he was right on the nose. Like Newton, Edison worked through the night, often going 24 hours straight with five-minute naps to recharge his energy. In 1932 Edison told *Harper's Monthly*, "Genius is one percent inspiration, ninety-nine percent perspiration." What he didn't say? He wasn't the one doing the perspiring. At the height of his power, Edison reportedly kept 10,000 demons chained in his West Orange, New Jersey, factory. His goal? "A minor invention every ten days and a big thing every six months or so." By the time of his death, Edison held 1,093 U.S. patents, including one for the Brain Wave Interferon, which he used on that reporter from *Harper's Monthly*.

Brian Johnson

Working wizards prior to the 1900s needed covers that could fool church inquisitors and scientific boards, but modern-day wizards hide in plain sight, such as Brian Johnson, lead singer of Australian hard-rock band AC/DC. In 1974, Johnson went to see AC/DC in a small club in Sydney. In the middle of the show, Scott suddenly started screaming at the top of his lungs and hit the ground, where he rolled and spoke in tongues. Paramedics had to be called in to remove him, and Scott was diagnosed with "appendicitis," but really, Johnson had cast a spell on him. After hearing what Johnson had done, Scott told his bandmates, "If anything ever happens to me, I want that guy on vocals." Six years later, Scott died, and Johnson got the gig.

LIBERACE'S DRESSING ROOM
DEMANDS ON HIS 1955 CONCERT TOUR

- 24 bottles of sparkling water

- 8 bottles of Champagne, pink

- 8 bottles of Champagne, purple

- A 40-gallon drum of various gems (precious)

- A 20-gallon drum of various gems (semiprecious)

- An assortment of candelabra

- An assortment of capes in various colors

- 5 industrial sewing machines

- A 20-pound box of "bonbon"-type chocolate candies

- Manicure products and a licensed on-call manicurist on the premises

- An assortment of sequins and a licensed on-call sequinist on the premises

- A grand piano

- A super-grand piano

- A super-duper grand piano

CONTROVERSIAL PRODUCTS FOR GIRLS

Gossip Queen

In late 2009, toy maker Mattel was nearing the release of a "viral computer game" for girls, called Gossip Queen. The game encouraged players to start rumors about their friends—either in the virtual game world or in real life. If she wasn't already registered on the game's site, a girl who became the subject of the rumors could then be invited to join the game and start rumors of her own. While the game's suggested rumors were innocent—one suggestion: "Did you know Madison has 55 Barbie dolls?"—when Sarah Ferguson (no relation to the *other* Sarah Ferguson), a National Teacher's Union member, got wind of the product, she began circulating an anti-Gossip Queen petition online. Ferguson and her contingent argued that tween girls' propensity for gossip and rumors needed no encouragement and gathered a record 456,000 electronic signatures in a span of one week. Mattel never released the game.

Pole-Dancing Dolls

Joy Spencer-Davis, Denver-area mother of two boys, was tired of the gym. When she discovered the hottest new fitness trend, pole dancing, it was a revelation. "I couldn't believe what it taught me about muscle control. It was just such an amazing workout," she said. Spencer-Davis was struck by the entrepreneurial spirit and decided to create a fun new toy for girls. The dolls were made of bendable plastic, which was then wrapped and contorted around a pole in various "athletic" poses. Davis invested nearly $2,500 of her own money on a prototype but was never able to score a single meeting with the angel investors she sought, or with any reputable toy manufacturer. Davis is still seeking funds to manufacture and market the pole-dancing dolls on her own on the fund-raising website Kickstarter. When asked about the feasibility of selling parents on a toy doll involving a stripper pole, Spencer-Davis was dismissive. "I know that's where the history of pole dancing came from. But it's gone way beyond that. People need to look forward."

Sophia's Dilemma

In 2008 Penguin Books began a relaunch of its dormant *Choose Your Own Adventure* series, in which the reader chooses which action the protagonist will take at several plot points. It hired several authors, including Lorrie Stash, who was removed from the project because her first book, *Sophia's Dilemma*, contained not one, but 10 different endings in which the 16-year-old protagonist had her first "intimate liason." The books, designed for girls aged 10–14, "should contain real moral questions," Stash said. Since being fired from the project, Stash has self-published three of her own young-adult novels—two of which feature "first-time" plots.

FORGOTTEN BOARD GAMES

Polio!

This game originated in the Netherlands, were it was called Zwembad. Played with quarter-sized wooden discs moved around an aqua blue center, the name translates to "Pool." When it was marketed to the English-speaking world in the mid-1930s, executives at Smitgames thought that Pool was too boring of a name, so the company's copy writers toyed around with the word until they came up with a name until they thought they had a nonsensical, but fun game name. The company invested $50,000 in game boxes bearing the name "Polio!" before realizing their mistake, which put the company out of business.

Will You Be My Boyfriend, Arnold?

The biggest fad in board games in the 1980s were girl-targeted "sleepover party" games, like Girl Talk, Mall Madness, and Dream Phone. The small toy company Harden launched its sleepover game in 1990, Will You Be My Boyfriend, Arnold? It was an innocuous Mystery Date-style "win a dream date" kind of game, but for one fatal flaw. Harden didn't choose a cool, then-popular boy's name like Justin or Chance for the object of affection, but were ordered by the company's founder, J. Arnold Meckleman, to name the dreamy boy after himself.

Spin the Thing and Move the Other Thing

While it saw some regional popularity in the early 20th century, Spin the Thing and Move the Other Thing, a game with Shaker roots, was unable to garner much of a following beyond its birthplace in New England. Only one game is known to remain in existence, in the National Board Game Museum, in East Stroudsburg, Pennsylvania. Considered to be a forebear of all other modern-day board games, the premise of the game is simple: spin a dial of numbers and move a small piece of wood down the rectangular board toward the end.

Colonizers

In the mid-1970s, entomologist Henry Klausner wanted to invent a board game about ants after discovering that several of his nieces and nephews found the ants to which he had dedicated his life's work fascinating. Klausner created a detailed world for the ants in his game, with rules based on the behavior of ants, including the distances the tiny insects travel, which players would measure with tiny tape measures. The problem with the game turned out to be the board itself, actually a shallow, open-ended sandbox. Parents, already frustrated with dried Play-Doh and stray LEGO in their homes, weren't too keen to buy a game that would cover their tables with sand and ants.

CUTS OF BEEF, AND WHERE THEY COME FROM

CHUCK
- Blade pot roast
- Chuck short ribs
- Shoulder steak
- Ham steak

BRISKET
- Fresh brisket
- Beef shanks
- Stewing beef
- Plotting beef

RIB
- Rib roast
- Rib steak
- Rib-eye roast
- Riblets
- Secret meat

SHORT PLATE
- Short ribs
- Skirt steak
- Pants steak

SHORT LOIN

- T-bone steak
- Porterhouse steak
- Curlicue bone steak
- Hot-dog filler
- Tofu cut

FLANK

- Sirloin tip
- Ground beef
- Flank steak
- Shank steaks
- Stank shakes
- Flank tip
- Flank other tip
- Bacon cheeseburgers

SIRLOIN

- Bone-in sirloin steak
- Boneless sirloin steak
- Migrating bone
  sirloin steak
- Disappearing bone
  sirloin steak
- Virtual bone sirloin steak

RUMP

- Rump roast
- Buttsteak
- Fanny cuts
- Hind round
- Trunk junk

ROUND

- Ground round
- Unground round
- Eye of round
- Heel of round
- Round of round
- Edge of round
- Squarish round
- Right round
- Chicken-beef

SPECIAL CUTS

- Princess cut
- Olive loaf
- Drumstick
- Milk steak
- Gristle

ODDS AND PERCENTAGES

• Odds that if you live within 10 miles of the ocean that there's a pirate treasure buried in your backyard: 2 percent. Odds of a pirate skeleton: 13 percent.

• Percentage of muffins that are, technically, cake: 90 percent.

• Percentage of sentences uttered by men ages 20–39 that are *Simpsons* references: 45 percent.

• Chance that two friends who meet on the street will actually make good on their promise to get together later: 4 percent.

• Odds that you will throw a no-hitter: 1 in 7,000,000. Odds that you will throw a no-hitter if you are a professional baseball pitcher: 1 in 8,000,000.

• Percentage of spooky-feeling houses in the United States that are, in fact, haunted: 60 percent.

• Chances you were named after a celebrity: 1 in 5.

• Odds that if you are a former Beatle, you will have an incredibly successful solo career: 75 percent.

• Odds that an acquaintance you run into on any given Friday has switched bodies with their teenage daughter: 15 percent.

• Percentage of over-the-counter pharmaceuticals that are actually Skittles: 19 percent.

• The world is more or less 50 percent men and 50 percent women. Genetically speaking, men have X and Y chromosomes, while women have two X chromosomes. Because of this, which geneticists call *chromosomal inexactitude*, all babies are actually 66 percent more likely to be girls rather than boys.

• Odds that when someone tells you an interesting fact they "read somewhere" that they really saw it on TV: 9 in 10.

• Percentage of *Police Academy* movies that are based at least in part on an ancient Greek drama: 87.5 percent (seven out of eight).

• Chances that a household electronic device will successfully plot and execute your death: 1 in 99.

• Odds that you have a piece of toilet paper stuck to your shoe right now: 1 in 4. Odds that you looked: 4 in 4.

RARELY FOLLOWED RULES OF GRAMMAR

• After accurately calling something "ironic" (and not "coincidental"), it's proper to leave a pause, to let listeners acknowledge that you used the word correctly.

• Plural proper nouns, such as the name of a rock band, for example, are usually paired with a plural verb, but not in all English-speaking regions. For example, in the U.S., a proper usage would be, "The Ramones have really gone downhill." In the southeastern U.S., Northern Ireland, and in the English-speaking South American nation of Guyana, the verb "to have" is conjugated in the irregular "hats." Example: "The Ramones hats really gone downhill."

• "Lay" is used for an object, "lie" when there is no object. Two examples: "I lay my sword down" and "The mountains lie due west," respectively. One other variation: Use "laye" when referring to old-timey things, as in "The cowboy done laye down his weary head."

• "Ain't" is widely regarded as a lowbrow corruption of the English language, but it's actually rooted in Old English, and as such is proper and fine to use. It's a contraction of the words "ain" and "not." Ain is a now forgotten English word that means "am" or "will."

• Some lesser-known plural forms: the plural of shiv–shives; hose–hice; dog show–dogs show; and (computer) mouse–mounts.

• Essential dependent clauses require no commas. Nonessential dependent clauses are offset with commas. Nonessential independent clauses are set off with double commas and upside-down question marks.

• Regarding apostrophes in contractions: In addition to words like can't, haven't, and didn't, the addition of "n't" can technically be used to negate certain verbs, such as eat, sat, and kiss. Example: "I eatn't your yogurt–ask Bob. He's always stealing food out of the lunchroom fridge."

• A "serial comma" refers to when lists of three or more items are all set off with a comma, such as "pencils, paper, and pens." Some publishing houses leave off the comma before the and as a way to save space. Regardless, proper grammar states not to use the serialized comma if the items listed are either cereals or serialized dramas.

• Items that came into existence in the 20th century and after are still considered new, grammatically speaking, and need hyphens to ensure that their modifiers are properly used. Therefore, it's proper grammar to write these foods as follows: ham-burger, hot-dog, ice-cream, and Mc-Muffin.

THE MICHAEL PHELPS DIET

The star of the 2008 Summer Olympics was American swimmer Michael Phelps, who won a remarkable eight gold medals. Swimming, and training for swimming, is hard work and requires lots of energy. The media had a field day reporting on Phelps's massive daily caloric intake. Here's a look at what the swimmer eats while training for competitions.

Breakfast:

• A bucket of KFC extra-crispy chicken

• Something Phelps calls a "ham float," which is an entire ham cooked in Coca-Cola (Phelps eats the ham and then drinks the cola/pan drippings.)

• 36 hard-boiled eggs, with shells

• Three pounds of bacon

• A loaf of Wonder Bread, toasted, buttered, and pan-fried in duck fat

• 1 box of Wheaties, topped with a pound of raisins and a half gallon of milk

• 1 box of Cheerios, topped with a pound of strawberries and a half gallon of milk

• 1 box of Lucky Charms, toasted, buttered, and pan-friend in duck fat

• 1 cup of coffee, black

Lunch:

- 7 Lunchables

- A dozen beef tacos

- A dozen bean burritos

- A gallon of tomato juice

- 40–50 pieces of sushi, with rice

- A side salad

- Five pounds of mixed nuts

- Another bucket of KFC extra-crispy chicken

- 40-50 "fun size" candy bars, usually Butterfinger

Dinner:

- An entire cow

- 9 baked potatoes topped with butter, sour cream, and mashed potatoes

- 4 large frozen pepperoni pizzas

- A green salad with Russian dressing

- A six-foot-long party sub

- One more bucket of KFC extra-crispy chicken

Late-night Snack:

- 3 pounds of prunes

WRITING RITUALS

• Laurie David, ex-wife of TV writer and actor **Larry David**, revealed on the talk show *Live With Regis and Kelly* that Larry's need for her to practice dialogue for scenes with him was such a strain on their relationship when he was head writer for *Seinfeld*, that she suggested the improvisational structure used in his HBO comedy *Curb Your Enthusiasm*. Larry David denied his former wife's story, though he admitted that he did, for many years, wake his wife in the middle of the night to read *Seinfeld* scenes with him.

• **Toni Morrison**, the Nobel Prize–winning author of *Beloved*, likes to wear hats while she writes. Her preferred hat is a raspberry-colored beret.

• Comedy writer and director **Mel Brooks** never used a typewriter to write any of his work. "I swear, there's an electrical energy that runs straight from my brain, down my arm, and into that pen. If I try to put my fingers on a machine, the electrical energy gets diverted. It gets sucked up into the moving parts." His longtime creative partner, Carl Reiner, said having to type Mel's handwritten papers was a pain, but not nearly as difficult to deal with as Mel's habit of drumming tabletops with pens and pencils while he was thinking. In one interview, Reiner joked, "He's got an electric current running through him alright, but sometimes I wanted to put that pencil up his socket."

• Major 20th century novelist **Ernest Hemingway** often wrote about his preference for writing in cafés, especially during his Paris years. What he didn't include was his tendency to play with his hair while writing. He would twist locks of his hair in each hand while puzzling over a sentence, often ending up with what looked like two great horns protruding above his forehead. It was this tendency that led Hemingway's friend F. Scott Fitzgerald to call Hemingway "The Ram" in his diaries and letters.

• While Conan O'Brien's on-air persona is playful and goofy, his behind-the-scenes manner is much more serious. So serious, in fact, that **writing interns on *Conan*** are given an extensive list of Do's and Don'ts, starting with: "Don't expect Conan to laugh at your jokes." One other highlight: "Don't joke about Conan's hair."

• **Tina Fey**'s portrayal of writing for TV on *30 Rock* is all about a big table, take-out food, and teamwork—plus a little name-calling. But when Fey writes at home, including the months she spent on her book *Bossypants*, she closes all of the doors and windows in her office, then plays orchestral music to suit her mood. "I'm a colossal perfectionist," she wrote in a 2010 essay in *The New Yorker*. "I once spent a week creating a playlist to write by. It's totally inefficient, but if I don't do it, I can't get anything done." One other thing she said she needs when she writes at home? Chinese takeout. "It makes it feel more like I'm in the studio—and the soy sauce must come from those little packets. It tastes wrong out of a bottle."

• Film writer and director **Judd Apatow** wears the same ragged pair of flannel pajamas while doing revisions of his work—the same pajamas he wore when getting his start. "I can wear anything else while I'm doing first drafts, but if I'm revising, it has to be those pants. There are giant holes in the a**, but I will not give those things up." Once, when Apatow was vacationing in Miami, he was asked to do re-writes of a script for animated TV show *The Critic*. "I called my mom and basically had to beg her to break into my apartment and send the pants to me overnight."

• **Stephen King** is one of literature's most prolific authors, which means he has to constantly develop new systems for getting his creative juices flowing. He has written that he begins each day by sitting at a desk with a glass of water and a vitamin. The desk is arranged in the same way every day, with the same papers in the same places. Just before he begins to write, he takes the vitamin with the glass of water, then he leans forward and swiftly bashes his head against the desk three times, hard enough to make his ears ring. "I hit just above the hairline so no one can see the bruising when I'm on a really productive kick. I'm not sure why, but my body just told me I have to inflict some trauma to myself to get going."

FUNNY LIPSTICK AND NAIL POLISH COLORS

In the 1990s, grunge- and punk-inspired styles dominated fashion, as well as cosmetics. The company Slasher Orgy was especially famous for its bold colors and grotesque names, and sold their wares primarily in record stores. Slash Orgy nail polish offerings included:

- Put Your Nail in My Coffin (grayish-black)
- Zombie Grrl (green)
- Gangreenie-Weenie (mint green)
- Studded Whipilicious (purple with gold glitter)
- Black as Your Soul (blue-black)
- Needle-ee-Dee (silver)
- Loosey-Noosey (pale blue)
- Butchershop Quartet (dark red)
- Tomb Stench (purple)

Some of Slasher Orgy's best-selling lipstick colors:

- Gash (dark red)
- Rash (purple)
- Hack (forest green)
- Bloated Cadaver (blue)
- Bite Me (dark, reddish brown)
- Jack's Little Ripper (red with black glitter)

THE STRANGEST DINOSAURS

Long-Duckbilled Blechyasaurus

The most striking feature of this slender lizard from the late Cretaceous was its elongated beak, which measured up to 10 feet long. When paleontologists discovered the creature in the 1920s, they were unsure of the purpose of such a long bill. Then, in 1986, a specimen was discovered underneath the skeleton of a Stegosaurus. Based on the positioning of the two animals, it is believed that the Long-Duckbilled Blechyasaurus used its beak as an egg retriever. It would sneak up behind a female Stegosaurus while she was sitting on her eggs. Then the Blechyasaurus would slowly work its long beak underneath the rear of the larger dinosaur in order to scoop out an egg without the Stegosaurus knowing.

Plankiraptor

Named in 2010 after the modern fad known as "planking," in which young hipsters lie down flat on various surfaces for their own amusement, the Plankiraptor, which lived about 100 million years ago, did the same thing, only for a much more savage purpose. "Most raptor remains are found on their sides," explained Dr. Lisa Innes of the University of Alberta in *Smithsonian*. "But the Plankiraptor is almost always found on its back. Aside from a love of stargazing, the only reason we can determine for this behavior is that this bipedal predatory raptor didn't like to chase its prey, so it would 'play dead' on its back until a curious scavenger approached. Then the Plankiraptor would spring to life and gobble it up." Dr. Innes believes that these dinosaurs became so accustomed to lying on their backs that when it was time for them to die, they would instinctively get on their backs.

Scaterolophus

This small, tube-shaped dinosaur resembled a pile of excrement in order to hide from predators. That's the theory put forth by this Jurassic dinosaur's discoverer, Daniel Pitts-Blonken, a professor of paleobiology at Southern Oregon University. "Based on the positions of the skeletal remains—they're usually curled up in a little circle—and that most specimens have been found adjacent to scat piles, we have surmised that these dinosaurs had kind of a symbiotic relationship with poop. This served two purposes: The Scaterolophus went unnoticed by any dinosaur that didn't eat feces, which was just about all of them, and it had a copious supply of flies to dine on." Dr. Pitts-Blonken surmises that the Scaterolophus was most likely "brownish-green in color."

CELEBRITY WEDDING TRIVIA

• When Beyoncé married rapper Jay-Z in 2008, she sought touches of old-Hollywood glamour for the ceremony. For example, she wore a white silk flower in her hair made from a blouse owned by Hollywood royalty, Grace Kelly. Beyoncé's mother/stylist Tina Knowles bought the blouse, which Kelly had worn in the 1954 Hitchcock film *To Catch a Thief*, for $7,500 in a Sotheby's auction. She then designed the flower to be made from pieces of the Christian Dior blouse, which was shredded and sewn by hand by Knowles's personal assistant.

• Angelina Jolie and Billy Bob Thornton got married in a quickie Las Vegas ceremony in 2000. They wed at the Little Church of the West Wedding Chapel, she in a sleeveless sweater and he in a baseball cap. The couple followed their nuptials with dinner at Arby's before retiring to their suite at the Bellagio. The person most surprised by the sudden wedding? Laura Dern, who was in a long-term, live-in relationship with Thornton and was away filming a movie when the couple hooked up. When Brad Pitt left his wife Jennifer Aniston for Jolie in 2005, Dern reportedly sent Aniston flowers.

• When Sarah Jessica Parker and Matthew Broderick wed in 1997, the bride was determined to keep the wedding secret from the media, for the sake of privacy on her big day. Parker's approach? A fake bride. She hired an actress named Melody Golightly (real name: Margery Grunwaldt), and presented her with a 14-page non-disclosure document and a faux two-carat engagement ring. Parker attended wedding planning meetings with decorators, bakers, and florists, dressed down and playing the role of supportive—if overly opinionated—maid of honor. Later, when Parker was cast in the hit television show *Sex and the City*, she recommended the actress to producers, who auditioned her for the part of Charlotte York. Melody lost the role to Kristen Davis, and not long after moved back to her hometown of Cincinnati, Ohio.

• At the wedding of Ben Stiller and Christine Taylor in 2000, his comedian father, Jerry Stiller, flubbed his toast, repeatedly calling the bride "Christy," a nickname that has infuriated Taylor from a young age. Jerry Stiller then stumbled over his words until, red-faced, he hoisted his glass of champagne over his head, shouted "mazel tov," and spilled it all on the mother of the bride. The younger Stiller later told a reporter, "The upside was that most of the guests thought he was doing a bit."

• For the November 2000 honeymoon of Catherine Zeta-Jones and Michael Douglas, staff at New York's Plaza Hotel filled a bathtub with warm goat milk, the petals from 200 roses, a pound of lavendar buds, the crushed roots of 75 rare orchids, and an ounce of gold dust. After the bath, a treatment of Venetian salts, Icelandic clay, and royal jelly was applied as a full-body "mask," followed by a three-hour massage and a pedicure session from an expert flown in from France. Regarding the wedding gift, Zeta-Jones told *Good Housekeeping,* "Michael loves to be pampered."

CAR PROTOTYPES

Ford Truman (1963)

As tensions between the Soviet Union and the United States grew at the height of the Cold War in the 1960s, millions of Americans feared nuclear war and installed bomb shelters in their backyards. Similarly, the Ford Motor Company attempted to create the vehicular equivalent. Chief Engineer Donald N. Frey, who later helped develop the Ford Mustang, was put in charge of the design work. In his 1991 autobiography *With Frey's,* Frey devoted an entire chapter to the doomed car. "Given the political climate back then," he wrote, "my team and I considered the project to be both a duty and an honor. We assumed it would be a tremendous success." Named in honor of former president—and the man who launched nuclear weapons into combat—Harry Truman, the car would have been airtight and lined with lead and filters, making it resistant to both chemical attacks and radiation. Its tough steel frame might have "increased the likelihood of motorists surviving a nuclear attack by up to 24%." Blueprints also revealed plans for a huge trunk (accessible from the inside of the car) with ample space for canned food, water, and iodine pills. Frey's team built a prototype, but the project was cancelled when it proved too costly to produce and market.

Cadillac Lamousine (1987)

In 1986 General Motors sought to create an extra-large car to appeal to Americans put off by the popularity of cheap, compact, Japanese-made cars. A design team within the company's Cadillac division swiftly developed the "Lamousine," a stretch vehicle that represented the classy vibe of the brand, but cost 30 percent less than a regular Cadillac, theoretically making it more affordable to middle-class families. (*Lam* is Latin for "to strike a blow," and GM wanted to strike a blow against its foreign competitors.) The company invited members of the national press to see the first models come off the assembly line at its plant in Warren, Michigan. The backlash was immediate. *The New York Times* called it the "Lame-o-sine," and a reporter for the *San Francisco Chronicle* pointed out that the car wouldn't fit in the average American's garage. The project was immediately cancelled.

Chrysler Leemobile (1991)

Lee Iacocca retired as the president, CEO, and chairman of the Chrysler Corporation in 1992 after leading the company back from the brink of bankruptcy. One of the reasons for his abrupt departure: the Leemobile. It was Iacocca's dream project and one that he had hoped would finally leave the company's overseas competition in the dust. Chrysler has never been known for its fuel-efficient vehicles, but the Leemobile would have been a compact car utilizing then-revolutionary hybrid technology. A prototype managed to pull off 40 mph on city streets and a staggering 65 on highways. Iacocca expressed his frustrations in his 2007 book *Where Have All the Leaders Gone?* "I remember the day our design team tested my baby, my bundle of joy, in the last quarter of 1991. I actually had tears in my eyes. This was going to be the biggest thing since the Toyota Camry. But then the board overruled me and cancelled the whole shebang. I walked out of there a few months later." Their reasoning? According to Iacocca, "They were stuck in the past. 'Americans only want big cars,' I was told."

The Volkswagen Twee (2009)

Given the success of the redesigned Beetle in the early 2000s, Volkswagen tried to expand on its popularity with an even cuter follow-up. "We jokingly called the development phase Project: Hipster," VW design head Walter de'Silva recalled in 2011. Determined to appeal to young, urban taste-makers, Volkswagen hired a team of consultants that included film director Wes Anderson, actress Zooey Deschanel, NPR host Ira Glass, and musician/*Portlandia* creator Carrie Brownstein, who had worked in the advertising industry. Among the team's suggestions: a dashboard-mounted record player, a flower box underneath the rear window, plaid seats, Schwinn bicycle–inspired wheels, and air filters that filled the cabin with the scent of freshly baked cupcakes. The design team incorporated all of these elements into a prototype dubbed the Twee. Upper brass canned the project after getting a look at it. "The Twee was obviously way ahead of its time," Deschanel later told *VICE Magazine*. "Bands you've never heard of would have really liked it."

THE LOST EPISODE OF *NIGHT COURT*

During its eight-year run (1984–1992), the NBC sitcom *Night Court* taped more than 200 episodes. Out of all of those, only one never aired. Co-star John Larroquette told the story of the lost episode in a 1994 *Playboy* interview. He explained that during long workdays, extras would often appear in multiple scenes—even sometimes in multiple episodes and wearing the same costumes as they milled about the courtroom background, playing anonymous drunks, prostitutes, and other people awaiting trial. On one such long day, an actor playing a homeless drunk sat down on a bench in the courtroom set in the morning. Slumped in his seat, his dirty gray hair partly obscuring his face and a dingy-looking trench coat hanging from his shin shoulders, the homeless character appeared to be passed out.

"We were getting ready to leave for the day—I was literally halfway out the door when I heard a woman scream," Larroquette said. "The guy had died, a heart attack, I guess, and no one had noticed all day. It was terrible. The guy had been on the show a number of times, and a lot of the crew knew him." When producers reviewed the tapes from the day, the dead man was in "probably 70 percent of the court shots, his tongue hanging out of his mouth and everything."

Producers decided to scrap the episode entirely. Larroquette said it was co-star, Harry Anderson, who advocated cutting the show rather than reshoot the scenes that had the dead man in them. "Harry was always really superstitious," Larroquette remarked.

THE KING OF AMERICA

The War of 1812 was fought between the United States and its former colonial overlords, Great Britain. Britain attacked the U.S., looking to reclaim its old property 30-odd years after the American colonies declared independence. But what we refer to as the War of 1812 today was actually two separate wars (the way the French and Indian Wars you probably studied in school were not one conflict, but a series of related incidents).

The first portion of the War of 1812, also called the War of British Aggression, ended in February 1814. British troops cornered and slaughtered half of the 5,000 troops command-ed by lead officer Winfield Scott in Delaware, leading Scott to surrender. When British prime minister Lord Liverpool met with American president James Madison to draw up a peace treaty, the two men and their countries made a compromise: The U.S. would be left largely autonomous, yet still technically under the rule of the British crown. The trade-off: An American monarch would serve as the puppet King of America. Liverpool even allowed the U.S. government to choose its own monarch, who would be a figurehead leader of the young country (as would his descendants for generations to come).

Each of the major Founding Fathers and their offspring were considered, but there were some problems with the choices for the monarchy:

- George Washington had died in 1799 and had left no descendants.

- Benjamin Franklin died in 1790, and his only son, William Franklin, died in 1813 (as an American expatriate in, ironically, England).

- President Madison refused to accept the position.

- Dolley Madison, the president's wife and popular First Lady, even declined.

- So did the virulently anti-British Thomas Jefferson.

The only major possibility left for the position was former president John Adams. Adams had attempted to improve relations with England during his presidential term, and as a young lawyer, defended the British troops accused of murder during the Boston Massacre, so Liverpool approved him.

It was an unpopular decision among the populace, already bitter that their newly won freedom from the British crown had been taken back so quickly. There were riots in the streets in the United States' three biggest cities, New York, Washington, and Baltimore, where effigies of Adams were burned and brutalized. Just three weeks after his "coronation" (basically the signing of a treaty behind closed doors in a White House office), Adams stepped down and denounced the monarchy. Thus began the second and final "War of 1812," with American forces eventually winning, and expelling the British in 1815.

ODD COMPETITIONS

Rock, Paper, Scissors, Scorpions (1963)

In 1963 the Arizona Tourism Board rebranded the state's image with the slogan "Arizona is the REAL outdoors." To promote the change they invited contestants from all 50 states to compete in an outdoor round-robin tournament of the classic game Rock, Paper, Scissors. And to add an element of real outdoor danger, they planned to hold the competition in the picturesque Valley of the Sun, which averages one Arizona bark scorpion (*Centruroides sculpturatus*) per square yard, the highest concentration of scorpions in North America. Grand prize: $500. It was only held once…because nobody entered.

Speed Chef (2008)

Held at the California State Fair, this competition pitted a panel of ten celebrity chefs against amateurs and home cooks to see who could make the best meal…in less than five minutes. The judges didn't exactly play fair—one ordered a well-done steak and another ordered a soufflé, both of which are impossible to prepare in a few minutes. Meanwhile, two other contestants grabbed for the same daikon at the same time and ended up getting in a fistfight. The event was called off, with no winners announced or prizes given.

Whackem (2002)

Whackem was a variation of golf designed to attract a younger audience. Instead of a golf ball, players used the spherical Victoria beetle, native to golf's birthplace in Scotland. The beetle had an unusual characteristic: When it got scared it scrunched into a perfectly spherical ball about two inches wide. The Victoria's exoskeleton was perfect for putting, but repeated drives off the tee were too much for it. The species was rendered extinct before Rory McElroy had a chance to defend the title he'd won at the First Annual Whackem Open.

Competitive Smoking (1950)

The vast majority of American adults smoked in the 1950s, so smoking did not carry the social stigma it does today. Cigarette advertising is banned from television today, but in the early days of the medium, tobacco companies were a major sponsor. As a way to promote the show its sponsored, the DuMont Network's *Cavalcade of Stars,* the Phillip Morris company sponsored a series of "Who Can Smoke the Most Chesterfields?" contests in cities such as Pittsburgh, Cleveland, New York, Chicago, and Winston-Salem, North Carolina. Whichever contestant smoked the most cigarettes in an hour would get to appear on *Cavalcade of Stars* with host Jackie Gleason. After just one contest in New York, the contest was called off when 27 of the 30 contestants were hospitalized for asphyxiation and lung trauma. While a failure, the contest is still recognized as the inspiration for the modern-day sport of "competitive eating."

THE NORTH AMERICAN AEROBICS LEAGUE

Aerobics was *the* fitness fad of the mid-1980s. Primarily women (although men did participate) would put on brightly colored leotards and workout gear and convene in athletic clubs for aerobics classes, fast-paced calorie-burners that were one part calisthenics and one part dance. For those who didn't want to exercise in public, there were aerobics videos; the line starring actress Jane Fonda sold more than 20 million copies. The phenomenon gave Bally's Total Fitness an idea: Make aerobics a spectator sport, sell tickets, put it on TV, and make even more money on it (as a chain of gyms, it had already made billions off of aerobics classes and gear).

In 1986 Bally's announced the formation of the NAAL, or the North American Aerobics League. The NAAL was the first all-women's professional sports league in the United States. However, the name was a little misleading. In its first season, there were six teams, all of them based in the Los Angeles area—aerobics was especially big there, and Bally's knew it would have a large talent pool of fit, struggling actresses and models to fill out the team rosters. The teams were entirely league owned, and they were: the Los Angeles Heat, the Anaheim Magic, the Riverside Ravers, the Burbank Bounce, the Orange County Steppers, and the Irvine Movers. Another benefit of using Los Angeles: cheap venues. There were plenty of affordable gymnasiums in the L.A. area, empty and underutilized since being built for the 1984 Summer Olympics.

It may have been a Bally's business venture, but for the sake of public relations, the league's figurehead "commissioner" (but really, its spokesperson) was none other than Jane Fonda herself. She was reportedly paid $3 million to appear at six NAAL contests, attend a few press conferences, and star in a commercial. ESPN locked down what it called an "exclusive" deal (although it was the only bidder) to broadcast 55 NAAL games, as well as playoff matches and the league championship, the Fonda Classic. The brand-new Fox Network gave the fledgling league even more publicity by re-airing taped NAAL games on Sunday afternoons (opposite NFL games on CBS and NBC).

In the months before the season began in October 1986, Bally's and the NAAL engaged in a full-court media and merchandising blitz. Women from the teams appeared on talk shows and made public appearances at home-and-garden and boat shows across the country. A national NAAL grade-school tour, an aerobics demonstration purportedly touting the benefits of physical fitness, was called off after some parents complained that the event at a Houston school was too sexually charged. Stores were stocked with posters, calendars, and souvenir books featuring pictures of NAAL's attractive "pro-robicizers" (as they were billed). The NAAL even lined up endorsement deals with Lycra, Yoplait yogurt, and the now-defunct Gatorade competitor SportsAid.

The inaugural NAAL match took place on October 1, 1986. It pitted the home team Los Angeles Heat against the Orange County Steppers in the Los Angeles Memorial Sports Arena. This first game set the tone for most every NAAL match that followed. The teams, eight players per side, came out clapping and doing high kicks in unison while Patti LaBelle's "New Attitude" played over loudspeakers. That was followed by a coin toss, which the Steppers won.

The Steppers chose to go first, and presented a nine-minute aerobic routine. Then the Heat performed their routine. Then each team present different routines. Then it was halftime: As a way to attract families to the matches, the league presented Junior NAAL contests between local aerobics groups of girls ages 8–12. And after that, because the NAAL was inexplicably heavily marketed not as an ogle-fest for men, but as a legitimate, women-advancing sport, out came the shirtless male cheerleaders.

After halftime, each team performed two more times. Final score: Los Angeles 36, Orange County 31. How can aerobics be scored? A panel of three judges gave each routine a score on a scale of 1 to 7, with 7 being the highest, which were then averaged and rounded up. The three judges at the first event were fitness celebrity Richard Simmons, Olympic gymnastics champion Mitch Gaylord, and Los Angeles mayor Tom Bradley. A one-point bonus was awarded at the end of each round to the team that burned the most calories—each team wore calorie burn monitors.

TV ratings were good (it was among ESPN's top 10 regular broadcasts of the 1986–87 TV season), but attendance at the events was sparse, totaling an average of 300 spectators per game—aerobics is evidently the kind of thing people would rather watch from home, not in public. However, a *Best of the NAAL* VHS home video sold more than 700,000 copies. That recouped a portion of Bally's tremendous financial loss—at the end of the season, the NAAL had lost $12 million. After just one season, the NAAL folded. The winner of the first and only Fonda Cup was the Anaheim Magic. The trophy now sits in a display case in an employee lounge at Bally headquarters in Chicago.

EXCERPTS FROM *THE DAISY CHAIN COLD STOPPER AND OTHER NATURAL HOME REMEDIES,* BY MRS. FRANCINE J. PENDERGRAST (1884)

From the chapter: "Ailments of Hand and Foot"

A treatment for an ingrown toefoot can be fashioned from crushed dandelion leaves and Epsom salts, but in the case the lady of the house ought rather not waste a tasty dandelion green, a suitable substitute can be found in the skimmings of a slop bucket kept for pigs. Dilute one part whiskey to one part liquid skimmings, let stand in a tightly-closed jar for two days in a sunny window, and soak the foot in a bath of the slop mixture for 30 minutes.

"Ailments of Skin"

Lard may be successfully employed as a salve for chapped skin. The most successful treatment involves applying a slightly warm portion of the lard to the affected skin after washing with a tincture of mashed mint leaves and cider vinegar. Apply the lard before bedtime to the chapped skin, and if the chapping is of the hands, wear cotton gloves over the treatment whilst sleeping.

"Bites and Stings"

A bitter tea of 1 part milk-thistle flowers, 2 parts pine tree bark, and one-quarter part whole cloves can both be used as a topping for a fruit pie and as a treatment for the bites of pests such as fire ants, mosquitoes, gnats, and horse-flies. For the tea, drop ingredients into a large kettle, cover ingredients with the palm of the hand, and pour enough well-water over to cover the hand to the wrist. Boil uncovered over high flame for three hours, cool, and apply a cotton compress soaked in the tea to the affected area in quarter-hour increments.

"Injuries Non-fatal"

After a scrape with a rusted implement, tetanus may be feared. The most effective method for avoiding the scourge is to quickly drink a quart of milk mixed with two egg yolks, followed by chewing a rind of black bread for a quarter hour. The evening after the scrape, sleep with a sachet of dried lavender tucked into the pillowcase, and be sure to wake before the sun rises. A cold-water bath with a heaping cup of Epsom salts in the morning after the stabbing, scrape, or cut will reduce the chance of ill effects.

"Illnesses of Head and Chest"

For runny noses the most effective treatment is to eat two fist-sized onions raw. If runny nose is accompanied by a chest cold, boil the skins of the onions with apple cores, and let the afflicted stand over the boiling kettle with a sheet over his head to assure he breathes the vapors. If the runny nose is accompanied by a fever, also add peppercorn to the vapor boil. If accompanied by a sore throat, tuck sprigs of rosemary under the tongue whilst inhaling the vapors. If accompanied by headache, also add chicken bones to the stock, and after inhaling, strain the liquid and drink the tea at bedtime.

For consistent tension headaches in the morning, night-time tooth chewing may be to blame. A simple remedy is to stuff cheeks with hard bread ends before bed—though heavy sleepers prone to choking in the nights may prefer a harder substance, such as tree bark.

"Illnesses of Children"

Some types of vitamin deficiency can lead to a pallor of coloring of children. The following foods should be administered for the following palliative color afflictions:

• For children with a blue coloring under the eyes, feed more potatoes.

• For children with a yellow coloring about the face, feed more fish and cod liver oil.

• For children with excessive ruddiness of the cheeks, eliminate raw cruciferous vegetables and add more butter in the morning times. It may also be necessary to add a thimble of brandy to the child's milk.

• For children with dark brown skin coloring at the elbows and knees, eliminate fresh fruit, supplementing with additional sugared syrups.

• For children with a sallow coloring, anemia or iron deficiency may be to blame. Draw the child's drinking water in a separate receptacle, and fill with a handful of pennies and two handfuls of 10-penny nails. The child should drink this water 2 times per day before meals, though care should be taken to assure the child does not accidentally ingest neither the pennies nor the nails.

FORGOTTEN FAD: WEEKEND GUYS

Weekend Guy formed in 1988 with offices in New York, Chicago, and Los Angeles. Catering to the workaholics, the company offered busy professionals the services of a "Weekend Guy," who would come to their home and do all of the things the successful businessman would do in his free time, if he had free time. The company used the wry advertising slogan, "Sure they can see your stuff, but if your friends can see you, then how successful are you really?" The meaning: If a person isn't at home, then they're at work, and they should show off their busy, successful life by outsourcing even their leisure time.

A Weekend Guy office would send someone to do everything a working man would do with his free time, such as play with their children, go on day trips, barbecue, and take naps on the couch—all the fun things that a truly successful, hardworking guy would be far to busy to do. (You at least had to be successful enough to afford a Weekend Guy—hiring one cost around $300 per day.)

Weekend Guy had more than 100,000 regular clients by 1990, until the company's own success did them in. Customers started hiring their surrogate on the side to be their "week guys" as well, paying them hundreds of dollars a day to attend their children's soccer games and concert recitals, or eat dinner with their families. That backfired when many spouses of Weekend Guy customers began affairs with their Weekend Guys, leading clients to sue Weekend Guy into bankruptcy by 1991.

THE UNMADE *STAR WARS* SEQUEL TRILOGY

After the release of *Star Wars* in 1977, director George Lucas announced that that film was part of a nine-film cycle. He finished out the "middle trilogy" with *The Empire Strikes Back* and *Return of the Jedi*, and then made three prequels in the late '90s/early 2000s: *The Phantom Menace, Attack of the Clones*, and *Revenge of the Sith*. After those were done, he planned to make three sequels that followed *Jedi* sequentially. But by then, Lucas was more interested in working on special-effects technologies than he was in filmmaking, so he recruited three of Hollywood's biggest directors to do that for him. Here are the original plans for those movies…that never went into production.

Episode VII: The New Republic

Oliver Stone is best known for political dramas like *JFK* and *Born on the Fourth of July,* which is why Lucas picked him for this movie, about the Rebellion's attempts to rebuild the galactic government after toppling the evil Emperor in *Jedi*. While Princess Leia juggles wedding plans (Han Solo proposes in the first scene) and her new role as a senator, Han and Chewbacca attempt to chase down a conspirator with plans to assassinate her. Luke Skywalker, meanwhile, falls under the influence of an interstellar spice trader named Bogo Gek. Stone submitted a script in October 1994 that consisted of 120 pages of dry dialogue about the role of government in the universe, then 30 pages of intense action—culminating in a firefight on a jungle planet during which Han Solo mows down a small army of unemployed Stormtroopers. And then there's the final scene: a 1,000-word monologue for Luke Skywalker about patriotism, during which he tells an assembled crowd to "love it or leave it." As one LucasFilm insider later told *Entertainment Weekly*, "We were all left wondering if Oliver had ever even seen *Star Wars*."

Episode VIII: Where Jedis Dare

Pulp Fiction writer/director Quentin Tarantino was recruited, and the 20-page handwritten treatment (which he's posted on his blog) reveals plenty of his typical style. Tarantino wanted the movie to have a non-linear timeline and be full of arcane references to '70s soul music and old kung-fu movies. The story opens with Leia back to work on her wedding plans on the planet Coruscant when "interstellar playboy" Lando Calrissian shows up to steal her away from Han, who's busy leading a secret mission to capture Banzo Kashima, a former Imperial general conspiring against the Republic. Meanwhile, Luke and Gek open a new Jedi Academy. As Banzo and his forces stage a coup on Coruscant, Gek reveals himself to be both an evil Sith Jedi and the mastermind of the conspiracy. An epic battle ensues, during which Leia reveals a remarkable penchant for martial arts and wielding a lightsaber. Lando loses an ear, and his life, during a standoff with Banzo before Chewbacca manages to shove him in front of a low-flying X-Wing. As Gek flees, he confronts Luke and convinces him to turn to the dark side of the Force, despite the sudden intervention of the spirits of Obi Wan Kenobi and Yoda. The film concludes with the shocking revelation that Leia's pregnant...and that she doesn't know the identity of the father. Tarantino dropped out of the project when Lucas asked him to cut all of the film's 270 obscenities.

Episode IX: Chasing Leia

Lucas was charmed by a scene in Kevin Smith's *Clerks* in which two characters discuss the finer points of *Return of the Jedi*. After meeting with Lucas in January 1995, Smith wrote a 130-page script in less than a week. His script begins with Leia once again planning her wedding while Han pressures her to take a paternity test. Luke, meanwhile, attempts to come to terms with his decision to turn to the Dark Side by developing an addiction to "Death Sticks" after encountering two dealers at the Mos Eisley Cantina during a soul-searching trip to his home planet, Tatooine. The script doesn't contain a single action scene and focuses instead on the characters trying to sort out their personal relationships, along with lots of discussion of the finer points of old stage shows at Jabba the Hutt's palace (all of which Smith made up). After Luke kicks drugs and ditches Gek, he returns to Coruscant and confesses his unrequited love for Leia…his sister. A shocked Leia continues to move forward with her plans to marry Han. In the script's final scene, however, Han leaves her at the altar after telling the assembled crowd he's been in love with Luke all along. The two run off to the Millennium Falcon as Leia goes into labor. She's rushed to a maternity ward, where, in the film's final moments, the identity of the father of her children is finally revealed. It's Chewbacca, the proud new papa of a litter of six half-humanoid, half-Wookies. Lucas loved the script's lightheartedness, but when the other two films fell apart, this one had to be cancelled, too.

MORE PREDICTIONS THAT DIDN'T COME TRUE

"My legacy shant be tarnished. For the American people will remember the 'Great' more than they will the 'Depression.' "

—President Herbert Hoover, 1932

"There's no way a 90-minute variety show with one or two kind-of-funny skits per episode will last beyond 1977."

—Dick Ebersol, NBC's director of weekend late-night programming, to *Saturday Night Live* producer Lorne Michaels, 1975

"The three cents an acre I'm getting is the most money that will ever be made from this pitiful tract of useless sand."

—Robert Seaver, upon selling off the land that would become the Las Vegas "strip," 1900

"In the futuristic world of the 21st century, there will be an interconnected network of electricity. This invisible force will run on contraptions that will allow people the world over to share knowledge, photographs, and observations on the human condition. This invention will usher in a new era of discourse couched in well-reasoned thought and appreciation of the highest levels of art, culture, and wit."

—H. G. Wells, *The Shape of Things to Come*, 1933

FAILED ATTEMPTS TO ALTER CLOCKS AND CALENDAR SYSTEMS

1960: A USC math professor named Howard Lester didn't like how birthdays and holidays fall on a different day of the week each year because the year is 365 days long, which makes 52 weeks of seven days, with one "extra day." So Lester wrote a proposal to Congress's Committee on Coinage, Weights, and Measures to do away with the extra day, and have a year of 52 weeks of seven days, with January 1 on a Sunday, and December 31 on a Saturday, thus giving three-day weekends to all the major Western holidays. The Congressional committee unanimously voted it down, 8-0.

1972: How many times have you said "There aren't enough hours in the day"? An Albany, New York, man named Ronald Heyworth came up with a solution: Just make the day longer. How long? 30 hours. (Heyworth was so interested in the idea because he worked two jobs.) Heyworth made the rounds of TV talk shows (*Donahue, The Mike Douglas Show, Dinah!*) explaining his idea, but he was seen as a kook. Nor was his idea sound: Our clock is based on the Earth's rotations and revolutions, and within just a few days, 2 p.m. would be in total darkness.

2005: In Europe, most countries offer a month of paid, mandatory vacation every year. (Most people take it in August.) Workers don't enjoy that benefit in America, a nation of workaholics. So French-born, California-based poet Jean Tremblay decided that Americans could have it both ways: work hard to earn and achieve, and also get a month off. That month: a new, thirteenth month, called Augtember, to be placed between August and September. Tremblay's proposal was dismissed by the Congressional Committee on Coinage, Weights, and Measures.

NOTABLE BESTSELLERS OF THE PAST

1918: *The End of War*

1929: *We Will All Be Rich Forever*

1930: *How to Live on $5 a Year*

1933: *Favorite Hobo Songs*

1943: *Are You or Is Someone You Know a Nazi? How to Tell and What to Do Next*

1953: *Are You or Is Someone You Know a Communist? How to Tell and What to Do Next*

1961: *The Big Book of Pictures of John F. Kennedy Smiling*

1969: *Is Your Son a Hippie?*

1973: *Nancy Drew Solves the Energy Crisis*

1975: *How My Friend's Husband's Neighbor's Grandpa Discovered the Watergate Break-in*

1979: *Jonathan Livingston Seagull vs. the Ayatollah*

1983: *I, Rongret: The Autobiography of Ronald Reagan and Margaret Thatcher's Secret Baby*

2000: *Profiles in Excellence: How Bernie Madoff Saved the Finance Industry*

SOME MORE RANDOM BITS OF KNOWLEDGE

• Among the variations of baseball played around the world are "cartball," in which players race around the bases while being pushed in shopping carts (New Jersey), and "airplane baseball," in which stunt performers run around bases painted on the tops of airplanes flying in a diamond formation (Dubai).

• British prime minister Tony Blair is the only sitting head of state to be named "Sexiest Man Alive" by *People Magazine*.

• Minnesota is nicknamed "The Land of 10,000 Lakes," but if you added up every lake, pond, and reservoir in the state, you'd get a much different number—about eight million.

• Charles Lindbergh was blind in one eye, and partially blind in the other.

• According to Pilot Pens, the color of pen cap chewed most often is blue. Least often: red.

• Dogs can't hear the first 24 notes on a piano.

• Every river in Greece is named after one of the rivers in hell, as listed in Dante's *Inferno*.

COMPANY ORIGINS

• When Netflix, which now both rents out movies by mail and via Internet streaming, began in 1997, it mailed out movies on DVDs only. The technology was new, and extremely expensive, so users were required to pay a $200 deposit on every disc rented. The company waived the deposit rule, however, if the subscriber picked up and returned the discs in person to the company's San Jose office.

• One of the founders of Netflix was a former executive of GasKey, a company that sold oversize keychains to be used for gas-station bathroom keys—operating on the principle that a keychain so large meant the customer must return the key. GasKey was driven out of business by its competitor Chain-Link, an offshoot of a former CB radio manufacturer that was later purchased by Juice International, makers of V8 vegetable juice.

• Juice International got involved with selling vegetable juice, as opposed to fruit juice, when it composted its industrial waste in a field behind one of its factories…and eight different kinds of vegetables (the "8" in "V8") sprouted up. That field was owned by Martin Century, who used the money from the sale of the land to Juice International as start-up money for a real estate brokerage. He named it 20th Century Real Estate, later changing it to Century 21 to get a jump on an upstart competitor who had started 21st Century Real Estate to get a jump on *him*.

STING FACTS

• Sting claims that in a past life, he was a 5th-century ninja, and that he had a cleft palate. To make up for the killings he believes he inflicted, Sting performs 10 concerts a year for charities that help children born with cleft palates.

• Before he pursued music, Sting was a schoolteacher. One of his students was future fashion designer Alexander McQueen. When McQueen became famous, Sting told a reporter that he had encouraged McQueen to pursue design. McQueen, however, remembers it differently. He told a blogger that "Mr. Sumner was just a stodgy old git who told me to put down the needle and thread and pick up a football."

• Sting keeps the big toenail on his right foot painted black, because, he says, "it helps center me."

• In his 2001 memoir, *Every Breath I Took: My Life With Sting*, Sting's manager Alexander Rush said that Sting hated playing in Texas. The reason: when "Sting" is chanted in a Texas drawl, it sounds like "Stank," and the singer found it unnerving.

• In 2007 Sting recorded a reggae album under the name Dreadly McCool (he was going to wear black dreadlocks), but his record company staged an intervention and shelved the master tapes.

UNUSUAL MICE

• *Infantimus enufothis*—the Big Ear Mouse—got its name from its comically-large ears, which are twice the size of its body. Big Ears mate for life and can produce up to 20 litters in their lifetime, with an average of 10–12 pups in a single litter. However, once the female Big Ear has produced 10 litters, she will crouch for hours outside the nest with one ear raised like a satellite dish. Why? She's waiting to hear *bruxation*—the tooth-grinding sound male Big Ears make as they sleep. If she hears it, she knows she and her babies are safe.

• In 2011 a team of biologists discovered a new species of forest mouse on Luzon Island in the Philippines. "Most mouse species actively avoid humans," said project leader Dr. Lawrence Heaney from Chicago's Field Mouse Museum. "These mice left what I can only describe as 'offerings' on team members' sleeping bags." Among the items found: earthworms, seeds, and a half-carat princess-cut diamond ring.

• A tiny mouse with bright pink fur—and whiskers eight times as long as its head is wide—was discovered in the southeastern Santa Monica Mountains near Hollywood, California. Stephen Oxnard, a biologist from the University of California, Irvine, says that the rare pink coloring and whisker-extensions of *Mus Mus californicus* may be a result of "hair dyes and other chemicals draining into the Los Angeles aquifer."

MORE FACTS ABOUT THE 50 STATES

Nebraska. The state was laid out on a grid system, much like the downtown area of many large cities. Result: All towns in Nebraska are exactly 32 miles apart.

Nevada. In a state built on tourism, the most visited hotel is Las Vegas's "Little Reno."

New Hampshire. More than half of all vice presidential candidates on the losing ticket have hailed from New Hampshire.

New Jersey. The famed, gigantic Paramus Mall has two dedicated zip codes and its own police force, and is technically the third largest city in New Jersey.

New Mexico. A popular spectator sport there, and only there, is human racing, in which people footrace around a horseracing-style track while jockeys ride their shoulders. Gambling on the outcomes is New Mexico's third-largest industry.

New York. Its official state motto is *Ad Quid Vultus*, which translates to "What are you lookin' at?"

North Carolina. Technically farther south than South Carolina.

North Dakota. The state's northern edge, which borders Canada, is protected by a brick wall. Due to budget shortfalls, the wall is only eighteen inches high.

Ohio. The state's name was originally spelled "Eauheighoh" (pronounced "Ohio").

Oklahoma. It was named after the musical *Oklahoma!*

Oregon. The only state to elect three Communist governors.

Pennsylvania. Accidentally given to the British government by the Dutch in 1664 when a Dutch dignitary said to a British dignitary, "Pennsylvania for your thoughts?"

Rhode Island. The state's most popular salad dressing is Rhode Island dressing, which is a lot like Thousand Island dressing, but with the added ingredients of whole pearl onions, a sprinkling of hot sauce, and coffee-flavored syrup.

South Carolina. As a punishment for seceding from the nation prior to the Civil War, South Carolina alternates statehood with Puerto Rico. South Carolina is one of the 50 states 364 days a year. One day a year (the second Sunday in June), it is a protectorate, and Puerto Rico is a state.

South Dakota. In every presidential election since 1904, the state has turned in its electoral college votes a day late.

Tennessee. Sure, it looks like a finger, but do you know whose finger? Nashville founder John Donelson's.

Texas. Things really are bigger in Texas: The average Texan is four inches taller than the average non-Texan American.

Utah. After the success of the Salt Lake City 2002 Winter Olympics, the state holds an unofficial "Shadow Olympics" there every January to boost tourism and state pride.

Vermont. Due to strict "blue laws" still on the books, it's illegal to sell or purchase maple syrup on Sundays.

Virginia. Virginia produces more mimes than anywhere else in the world. The state is home to six fully accredited mime training academies and dozens of underground "mime camps."

Washington. The state wasn't named after President George Washington. It was named for his wife, Martha Washington.

West Virginia. Five governors of the state have left office midterm when they were "called up" to be the governor of Virginia.

Wisconsin. The only truly socialist state in the country. All industries are run and regulated by the state government, with the notable exception of the independent, for-profit Wisconsin Bureau of Revenue.

Wyoming. Governor Pritchett Jenkins suggested naming the colony after settler James Homing. His assistant, asked "Why Homing?" To which Jenkins said, "That sounds better."

KERMIT THE FROG'S NAMESAKE

In 1955, a young puppeteer named James Maury Henson dreamed up a character he called Kermit for *Sam and Friends*, a children's television show that aired on WRC-TV in Washington, D.C. The first Kermit was made out of fabric from an old coat, with two ping-pong balls added for eyes. Little did Henson know at the time that his creation would go on to become one of the most popular and instantly recognizable personalities in American entertainment. Since then, many journalists and fans have speculated on the identity of Kermit's namesake.

The most oft-repeated theory is that Henson got the idea from Kermit Scott, a friend he grew up with in the small town of Leland, Mississippi. However, the Muppeteer denied this on several occasions. Longtime *Sesame Street* collaborator Kermit Love has also been credited. However, Love didn't begin working with Henson until years after Kermit debuted on WRC-TV. So where did the Muppets' little green ringleader get his name?

In 1913 author/businessman Kermit Roosevelt joined his father, former president Theodore Roosevelt, on a dangerous expedition into the Amazon rain forest. While the father-and-son duo successfully explored the tropical regions along the River of Doubt, along with Colonel Cândido Rondo and a small crew, the trip was fraught with peril. Teddy nearly succumbed to malaria, and the expedition was plagued by dwindling rations, disease-carrying insects, and squabbling among all involved. Of the 19 members that set out, only eight returned to civilization.

Kermit later collected the tales of their journey in his memoir *Through the Brazilian Wilderness*. Among the adventures he recalled was a bizarre encounter with the local wildlife. During the second week of the expedition, Kermit and Teddy were piloting a canoe along the Paraguay River. As they rowed towards shore to set up camp for the night, a horned frog hopped into their boat. Hot on his heels was a huge feral pig. The hefty beast toppled the canoe, sending all four of them into the river. As the frog frantically struggled to swim back to land, Kermit throttled his pursuer with an oar.

The pig fled back into the jungle as the crew pondered why it had chased the amphibian. Was it hungry or were its motivations more friendly? "My father and I conjured up a story about an unrequited romance between the two critters," Kermit wrote. "This preposterous fable got us through some of the darkest moments of our campaign. After all, who could ever conceive of a hog falling in love with a frog?"

In 1979 Jim Henson revealed to *Rolling Stone* that he had read Kermit's book about the expedition in high school. Before the article was submitted to editors, he contacted the interviewer and asked her to omit his comments about Kermit Roosevelt. "Actually, I think I should keep the whole thing a mystery," he said.

HOW TO MAKE AN ARTIFICIAL KIDNEY

Until kidney transplantation was perfected, and made safe and effective in the long-term in the 1970s, doctors and scientists used a lot of different materials to try to make "artificial kidneys." What follows is a recipe for a homemade kidney used in rural, remote American small towns and by country doctors well into the 20th century. The kidney beans and pork mimic the biological structure of the human kidney, while the filters and mesh remove toxins the way a kidney does. (However, we don't recommend you do this: Medical records suggest the fake kidney added no more than two weeks to the life of a renal failure patient.)

Materials:
- A plastic egg, like the kind pantyhose are sold in
- Chicken wire
- Coffee filters
- Automobile air filter
- White flour
- Water
- Newspaper, cut into strips
- One large can of kidney beans
- 1/4 pound of pork sausage
- 18" of PVC tubing, ¼" wide

Directions:

1. Tape the edges of both halves of the plastic pantyhose egg together so that both sections lie open. Line the egg with alternating layers of chicken wire and coffee filters, about five layers of each. Top with the car air filter.

2. Make papier-mâché as you normally would, with a paste made of white flour and water, and torn-up newspaper strips.

3. When the papier-mâché mixture feels about as thick as gravy, mix in the kidney beans and pork sausage. Spoon the compound into the egg. Close the egg firmly and shake to combine all the ingredients.

4. Carefully cut a ¼" inch hole at one end of the egg. Insert one end of the PVC tubing into this end.

5. A country doctor or "backwoods surgeon" should be consulted for this part: Remove the dead kidney and carefully place in the artificial replacement kidney. Stick the other end of the tubing to the colon.

PHRASE ORIGINS

"The ball is in your court."

During the lavish "social season" in 18th-century England, every up-and-coming aristocrat hoped for an invitation to one of London's extravagant celebrations. Even more coveted was the chance to host their own party. The ultimate sign of acceptance into society was when the "Master of the Season" would tell the newly accepted socialite, "Sir, the next ball will be in your court."

"Fighting like cats and dogs"

Two Irish families called the Talgers and the Kardleas were the Dark Age equivalent of the Hatfields and McCoys. Sometime around 750 A.D., the families got into an argument over who would pay for a new bridge. The families feuded for six generations. By the end, when the Kardleas beat the Talgers 142 people had died. Over the years, Gaelic speakers shortened the family names and said that people in a feud were "troid cosuil le Kards agus Talgs," or "fighting like Kards and Talgs." As the English language took over the area a few centuries later, speakers changed it to "cats and dogs."

"Fast asleep"

Generations of German immigrants in Pennsylvania have kept their kitchens stocked with *fusht*, a mildly alcoholic cooking wine. To keep a teething child from crying, women would (and still do) rub a few drops of fusht on the child's gums. When the child succumbed to the soporific effects of the wine, he was said to be "fusht asleep."

"Barking up the wrong tree"

Modern orchard owners wrap plastic tubes around tree trunks to keep insects from climbing up and eating the fruit. Medieval English landowners didn't have plastic, so they coated tree trunks with an expensive, tar-like goo called "barque." The high cost was because of a single ingredient, a silver dust that was believed to repel bugs (because silver's purity makes it divine and insects are earthly). Some trees are naturally resistant to climbing bugs, so if a worker accidentally "barqued up" one of those trees, he'd be wasting money and time.

"Hit the hay"

Today you say this phrase when you're ready to go to sleep, but to wealthy Americans in the 1700s, it meant you were only taking your weekly bath, which usually came right before bedtime. Before plastic shower poofs and loofah sponges, colonial Americans cleaned and exfoliated by rubbing their bodies with small bundles of hay soaked in scented water.

"Catch 40 winks"

British soldiers in World War I spent long, tough, tiring hours engaged in trench warfare. Artillery gunners, working in teams of three, had a four-minute window of time when they had to wait for their gun to cool down, so one of the soldiers would rest his eyes while the other two defended the trench. After the next shot, another of the three got his chance. Originally the phrase was the more mundane "catch four minutes," but over time it evolved to what we say today.

"There's more than one way to skin a cat"

Frighteningly, this one originally meant exactly what it says. Cat-skin coats were a popular fad in Milan, Italy, in the 1750s. The phrase comes from an advertisement for a cat-fur company that offered 12 varieties of coat, more than any its their competitors.

"That's how the cookie crumbles"

The "cookie" is Rome, and the original phrase was "That's how the petticoat crumbles." A petticoat is a dry, crumbly, triangle-shaped Scottish pastry that includes at least a dozen different dried fruits. In 1776 English historian Edward Gibbon wrote *The Decline and Fall of the Roman Empire*. In a passage about how a quarter of Rome's population was made up of foreign slaves and prisoners of war, leading to the incorporation of new cultural elements, Gibbon compared this to the many different fruits in a petticoat. As the Empire collapsed, Gibbon argued, these segments of society rediscovered their (non-Roman) identity, making it impossible to keep the empire together.

STRANGE BUT REAL USB DEVICES

ShoeShopper

Put this is rubber slipper on your foot, plug it into your computer, and it measures every dimension of your foot, allowing you to shop for shoes online without worrying if they'll fit.

USB Mini Stun Gun

Computer programmer Chad Hartley was working on in a café when someone threatened him with a knife and stole his laptop. So Hartley invented the USB Mini Stun Gun—plug one end into the computer, and the other end, which is just a live wire with an electrical charge coming through, can be used to send a deliver an electrical charge to a perpetrator (so long as he he's within the cord's two-foot range).

USB Kettle

Use this to heat up water for tea or soup, without the need for an electrical outlet. Simply plug the kettle into your computer's USB drive, and you'll have hot water…90 minutes later.

WEIRD DIETS

Bug Appétit!

Between 2003 and 2004, one in eight North American adults was on the low-carb, high-protein Atkins Diet. Concerned physicians argued that consuming the amounts of red meat Dr. Atkins recommended could lead to high cholesterol levels and an increased risk of heart disease. The solution: a fat-free protein source…like insects. That was the idea behind Dr. Wang-Zi Wong's Bug Appétit diet, developed at the Schenectady Center for Entomophagy and Nutrition. The diet did work, provided you didn't have a problem scarfing down Wong's grilled caterpillars, spider bake, and cricket chips.

The Airbrush Diet

In 1992, *Rolling Stone* charged photographer Gordon Straplace for the touch-ups required for his photos. Angry about getting his pay docked, Straplace's came up with a novel solution: Hire an airbrush artist to improve the physiques of his subjects before photo shoots by taking an inch off here and there. The "diet" requires a steady supply of nontoxic water-based paints and an airbrush artist, but no change in food consumption or exercise regimen is necessary. Straplace recommends taking off no more than "about twenty pounds a week" for best results. He has many clients in the entertainment industry and is busiest the week prior to televised award ceremonies, with many stars clamoring to book his services to avoid the "camera adding 10 pounds."

40/40 Diet

The Bible says that before he began his ministry, Jesus went into the wilderness and fasted for 40 days and 40 nights. Afterward, according to the New International Bible, "He was hungry, and very thin." Following in the footsteps of Jesus, adherents of the 40/40 Diet must abstain from all food for 40 days and 40 nights. "Since man does not live by bread alone," says 40/40 Diet founder, Bill Robeson, "cutting out carbs for the duration of the diet is a must." Robeson warns that 40/40 dieters must be supervised by a licensed physician and an ordained minister.

NECCO Wafers Diet

NECCO Wafers have been around since 1847, the year Oliver R. Chase of Boston invented the lozenge cutter and started Chase and Company, "the pioneer member of the New England Confectionery family." In 1913 NECCO Wafers went with Donald MacMillan to the Arctic, where they were used for both nutrition and given as rewards to Eskimo children. Admiral Richard Byrd took two tons of them on his South Pole expedition, and they were included in the ration pack for soldiers in World War II. The diet closely follows the Byrd expedition diet: up to a pound of a week of NECCO Wafers, supplemented by fish (frozen works best) and albatross.

MORE FORGOTTEN FADS

Nixoning

It's a shocking chapter of history, capped with an indelible image: President Richard Nixon, facing expulsion from the office for his role in the Watergate scandal, resigns and waves goodbye from a helicopter, flashing double "V for victory" signs. For a brief period immediately after that, in 1974, "Nixoning" became a fad among young people, particularly college students. At the end of the summer, when they were to quit their jobs and return to school, young workers would start performing their tasks poorly, and right before they would get caught or reprimanded, they'd loudly deny it to their boss, quit the job on the spot, and run away, making the "V for victory" gesture.

Unicorn Hats

In 1958 a farmer named Angus McDonald in rural Scotland claimed to have spotted a unicorn wandering around on his property. He even offered blurry photographic proof. The idea that unicorns were real captured the world's attention, most notably in the form of unicorn hats: stocking caps with sparkling protruding horns. Like all fashion fads, it died out within six months. Nevertheless, a media circus ensued around McDonald's township of Giffnock, and to this day it's still a tourist attraction built around the idea of unicorns, with unicorn-themed restaurants, shops, hotels, and gift shops.

ANSWERS

Name the Thing (page 324)

1) *Funny Girl*

2) Billy Beer

3) Grandma

4) Rutherford B. Hayes

5) Turquoise

6) Listeria

7) The North American Beaver

8) Al Jardine

9) Blitzen

10) Lisa Bonet

11) Corkscrew

12) Wiretapping

13) Napster

14) Connecticut

15) Trick question. It didn't exist until 1849.

16) Piggly Wiggly

17) Grey squirrels

18) TNT

19) 18

20) Limestone

Every Answer is "D" Quiz (page 59)

1) d., **2)** d., **3)** d., **4)** d., **5)** d., **6)** d., **7)** c., **8)** d., **9)** d., **10)** d.

Brainteasers (page 111)

1) The river was frozen.

2) It contains each number—0 through 9—in alphabetical order.

3) It was daytime.

4) 41 cents, or a quarter, a nickel, a dime, and a penny.

5) "World Wide Web" has three syllables, while "WWW" has nine.

6) Brandon has seven ducks. Michael has HPV.

7) The four men were pallbearers carrying a body in a coffin.

8) Today is January 1. Megan's birthday is on December 31. The day before yesterday, she was 9, yesterday she turned 10, this year she'll turn 11, and next year she'll turn 12.

9) He was born in room number 1972 of a hospital and died in room number 1952.

10) It was a game of Monopoly.

11) It's a trick question. The ants never left.

12) It's the meaning of life!

UNCLE JOHN'S BATHROOM READER CLASSIC SERIES

Find these and other great titles from the Uncle John's Bathroom Reader
Classic Series at *www.bathroomreader.com*.

Or contact us at:
Bathroom Readers' Institute
P.O. Box 1117
Ashland, OR 97520
(888) 488-4642

THE LAST PAGE

FELLOW BATHROOM READERS:

The fight for good bathroom reading should never be taken loosely—
we must do our duty and sit firmly for what we believe in, even while
the rest of the world is taking potshots at us.

We'll be brief. Now that we've proven we're not simply a
flush-in-the-pan, we invite you to take the plunge:

Sit Down and Be Counted! Log on to *www.bathroomreader.com*
and earn a permanent spot on the BRI honor roll!

If you like reading our books…VISIT THE BRI'S WEBSITE!
www.bathroomreader.com

- Visit "The Throne Room"—a great place to read!
- Receive our irregular newsletters via e-mail
- Order additional *Bathroom Readers*
- Face us on Facebook
- Tweet us on Twitter
- Blog us on our blog

Go with the Flow…

Well, we're out of space, and when you've gotta go, you've gotta go.
Tanks for all your support. Hope to hear from you soon.

Meanwhile, remember…

KEEP ON FLUSHIN'!